AlphaBetaPocalypse

By Sam Sobelman

For LDH

Your Alphabet Is The Best

AlphaBetaPocalypse

Hegemon Solomon woke in a cold sweat, panicking as his dream shattered into gray oblivion. Billions of terrifying beasts had been nipping at his heels, chasing him down a cobblestone street in an unfamiliar city. He had kept his tendons just a hairsbreadth away from being devoured in a most unpleasant fashion. Flashes of the devils' breaths raised his hackles and he shivered, despite the artificial warmth of his bedroom. The whole experience had been just a little bit too real to shake off as an everyday dream.

The Hegemon performed a quick search his bedroom, just to make sure he was safe from harm. He glanced under his bed, perused his wardrobe, and made sure the window was still latched. Nothing in his room was any scarier than usual. The tree outside his bedroom cast skeletal webbing on his floor and bedding, backed by a glowing moon. The stuffed clown his mother had given him ages ago still smiled grotesquely from on top of his bureau. The silver light of midnight reflected off of a picture of his past: him smiling in his mother's arms. His young grin shone from its usual bed, a frame placed next to the terrifying doll. Everything was in its right place, but he couldn't shake the chills from his dreamland experience.

One demon, the most terrifying of all, had been at the back of the pack, driving the umbral army before him. He was a great, black moose, as long as he was tall, with a shadowed crown of antlers as sharp as his teeth. A wild tongue lashed out at his minions like a whip, urging them onward toward their tasty prey, the Hegemon. All the beasts cried Solomon's name as they ran, beckoning him to slow for just a second and play with them.

Solomon hadn't been raised to accede to any demands besides his own. He was the Hegemon, after all. His special training at the secret Bureaucrat Academy had served him well; he had acquired the strongest will on the planet. Just one day ago he had negotiated a peace agreement between two muscle-brained heads of state fighting over a submarine sandwich. A few little nightmares should be nothing to him, now. His mother would have scolded him, if she knew how troubled he was by the dream. An overbearing Jewish mother, she would have given him some warm chocolate milk, nestled him in her busom, and sent him back to bed feeling guilty for having broken her slumber.

Nostalgia of his dear mother filled Solomon with a lost courage and warmth; the chills from his dream were finally dissipating. A glance at the moon revealed that the night was still in the witching hours; there was much sleeping still to be done. After one last, neurotic search of his room, the Hegemon crawled back into his bed, snuggled under the covers, and shut his eyes to get some rest.

After several sleepless minutes, he reopened his eyes and screamed. "Mother, may I!"

Looming above, inches from his face, was a mouth full of razor-sharp umbrage. The mouth was attached to a familiar face; a cold snout, molten eyes, and a jagged crown of shadows. The moose devil was standing on Solomon's bed, breathing noxious vapors into his gaping mouth. His nightmare had manifested into a vicious, corporeal beast.

"Your mother can't hear you now, Solomon," the moose rasped. His voice sounded like sandpaper rubbing flesh away from bone; his breath smelled the same.

"Buh, huh, mah," Solomon stuttered. "Guards! Security! Get in here! Help me!"

"They can't hear you either Hegemon, not here," the moose continued, "But you are safe, for the moment. I come to hold counsel, only. I cannot hurt you here unless you wish it."

"How can I trust you?" Solomon said, "You were trying to eat me in my dream! Your soldiers were going to tear me to pieces!"

"Yes," the moose hissed, "and that was a warning of what is to come, Hegemon. That is, if you choose to fight me and my will. I am coming to play a game in your world, Solomon. If you follow my rules, I might consider sparing your life."

"My life?" Solomon had sworn to give his life to save the world many years ago, when he first took his oath of office. But, that vow was only words, when it came down to it. "My life, well, you can't threaten me. I'm the Hegemon."

"A pretty title, to be sure. Many people respect your authority. However, I am not one of them. In fact, it's best if you don't think of me as a person at all," the moose smirked. "And it's not your life alone that you should be worried about. Think bigger, Hegemon. Imagine every spark of human life, extinguished by a single decision you might make. There's a choice you must make, my friend. You hold in your hands the destiny of human existence. Will you play for my team, Hegemon?"

Solomon gritted his teeth to stop them from chattering. "I refuse to negotiate with terrorists."

The moose laughed, a heaving tide of pestilence. "I am much worse than a terrorist, Hegemon. Or even a horrorist. Gods and hellspawn have got nothing on me. There are no words to describe how sickeningly scared you should be. Allow me to elaborate for a moment.

"All the beasts in your dream, the ones slobbering for your flesh, are hungry to feed. They are very real, at least as real as me. It is only a matter of time before I can unleash them to hunt down you and every other warm-blooded creature on your planet. The cold-blooded beasts will make soothing desserts to slake my army's parched throats." The moose's pink tongue was beginning to shine with thirsty saliva. "I designed them all with an insatiable taste for fresh plasma, Hegemon. They will drink until there is no more to swallow. I will ask you again, because I don't think you understood me the first time. Will you play with me or against me?"

Solomon gulped away his tongue's paralysis. He decided it might not be a bad idea to listen to this lunatic anthropomorph, at least for now. "Okay, moose. I will listen, b-but I'm not promising anything, yet. What would you have me do?"

4

" Oh, I'm so glad you're willing to listen. It will make things so much easier on the both of us," the moose smiled, drawing closer to Solomon's face. "I have a few simple requests."

Solomon could hardly breathe; the moose's toxic breath filled his lungs instead of fresh air. "Ask me, already. I'm listening."

"The first request, I think you will find quite disagreeable," the moose said. "At the Summit of Nations, in two weeks, there are a number of countries who are going to propose a motion to secede from the Hegemony. You must let them leave."

"You can't be serious! This will cause terrible repercussions. If I let them leave, countless others will ask to secede as well. The Hegemony will dissolve! The world will fall into chaos! Countries will be scrambling to assert their independence and will probably enter into meaningless war. The Hegemony was constructed to prevent this exact scenario."

"Precisely," the moose grinned. "It will be a beautiful disaster. I'm salivating just thinking about it. Don't you want to know what will happen? Don't you want to watch the world burn away?"

"Never! That goes against everything I've sworn to do. I gave my solemn oath to stand for order and justice! To protect the innocent from power hungry tyrants like you."

The moose laughed. "Well, you might stand for all that silliness, but you will still fall beneath my raging armies. You saw them in your dream. Do you really doubt my might?"

"I do not doubt your strength, sir moose, but you are asking me to make a decision as though all hope is already lost. Perish beneath your soldiers or lose ourselves to our own devices. I can't just give up hope at the drop of a hat. I've given my whole life to the cause of order and justice."

"And you will give it completely, if you resist me. You will sacrifice the life of every organism my dark knights encounter. Can you shoulder that guilt? Come now, Hegemon, be reasonable. Play with me, and I might go easy on your planet."

"But, my oath," Solomon stammered. "I, my, I promised. Mother, I, forgive me."

"Oh, don't worry about that. You can pass the blame off to another," the moose crooned. "In several week's time, you will be approached by the one who will replace you in your office. At this time you can be assured that I am walking the filthy ground of your planet. You will abdicate without resistance because, I assure you, any efforts to deny me will fail. This is my second request. I will not hesitate to annihilate every living creature if you try to balk me."

"Why is that? Is this an emissary of yours?" Solomon asked desperately, pining for answers. "Do you want to rule the planet or do you want to destroy it? I don't understand your motivation. Why are you here?"

"My reasons are of no concern to you, mortal," the moose crouched low and began to lick the Hegemon's neck with a virile hunger. "All you need to know is that standing against me will result in infinite death. Have I made myself clear? Do you need me to draw you a diagram? I have big plans for this universe. Your world is an incredible source of power, so I'm giving it my utmost attention, for now. What I end up doing with it is my perogative." His shivering tongue slithered up Solomon's cheek.

The Hegemon was on the edge of tears, a monolith shattered. "Please, what else do you want? Just ask me and leave me to my peaceful slumber. I can't take this anymore. I'll do whatever you ask."

"Poor little human, I have asked quite a lot of you, I realize. The final thing you must do is wait for me, your new master, to come embrace you. Spend your days fearing me and learn to worship that terror. It will prepare you for the ultimate transition into my kingdom of chaos."

"I promise!" Solomon sobbed. "I will give every waking moment to fearing your footsteps, mighty, oh, what should I call you, sir?"

"There is no need to burden you with that knowledge at this time. Besides, you must only ever call me Master," the moose said, licking Solomon's ear, sending an icy dagger through the Hegemon's soul. "The world will know my name when the time is right," he whispered, before ripping off his prisoner's ear with a terrific bite.

Hegemon Solomon woke in a cold sweat, panicking as his dream shattered into oblivion. The sun was shining and his alarm clock was blaring smooth jazz. He jumped out of bed to shut off the alarm and searched his room for any trace of the moose demon or his minions. Not finding anything suspicious, Solomon pinched himself to make sure he wasn't still dreaming. It had happened again, the dream within a dream. He fell into that trap every other night, with the same demons chasing him to a false awakening. The moose demon came every time and every time he nearly wet himself with fear, forgetting his previous encounters. It didn't seem right, that he could fall for the same trap over and over, but he did. He wasn't the superstitious type. He had no desire to understand dreams or study what they meant, but this recurring motif was really starting to bother him.

He went over to his bureau and picked up the picture of his mother, avoiding the disappointed stare of the smiling clown doll. He wished he could call her and ask her for advice. In truth, he knew what she would say. She would tell him that big boys don't cry, that if he wanted to grow into a strong man he should forget about it and get back to his work. Otherwise, he would never find a good woman. His mother, rest her soul, never understood that a Hegemon was not to be married under any circumstances.

Solomon sighed, wondering if these dreams were his subconscious mind's way of telling him to start a family. His waking logic told him that was just his neuroses speaking out of turn. Still, he knew these dreams were more than dreams; they were happening all too frequently. Today's dream had been more realistic than ever before, his level of lucidity had been horrific. Some kind of action needed to be taken. Solomon's will was fraying; he was losing touch with reality. Even if the nightmare army wasn't real, he wasn't fit to run the world anymore. Solomon put his mother's picture back, placing it face down on the bureau, and gathered some pens and paper.

The Hegemon looked out his window to see a yellow finch tweeting from its nest in the spindly tree outside. Solomon envied its joyous celebration of freedom, its lack of responsibility, its lack of fear. He sighed longingly. This was a good day to write an abdication speech.

Just in case.

Anonymous

Petyr crammed himself in a shadowed alcove, shrinking his presence until the only trace of his existence was a fiercely beating heart. Adrenaline coursed through his veins and tensed his bones. His eyes twitched with anxiety; he hoped the distraction he had planned would conceal him from the panicked eyes of his enemies. He ground his teeth together and prayed to the almighty unknown while he braced for endless waves of alarms to begin. Deep down, in the nebulous heart of his being, he prayed that all his problems would work themselves out.

Fate. Kismet. Karma. Destiny. There were endless names he could give to that intangible source of courage at his core. Though many people needed some sorts of crutch to keep themselves off the ground, Petyr had decided long ago that he would never bend his knee to a god. The highest power he worshipped was his own ability, but this dire situation was making his faith waver.

Sweat drenched his palms, suddenly as slick as a rainy curb. Petyr readjusted his grip on his prize; if he accidentally dropped the briefcase, the crash would echo throughout the facility and alert every slimy guard to his exact position. Certainly, if he were discovered he would be slaughtered on the spot; no quarter was granted in his line of work. If he managed to escape detection, he would probably lose himself in an attempt to escape. The mission had been a miserably planned minefield; it was either a miracle or blind luck that Petyr had acquired his target and survived to this long. If, through some grand twist of the universe, the rest of his plan were to succeed, Petyr hoped he would earn enough points for his boss to give him a long deserved vacation.

The game was called Anonymous and playing it was Petyr's true calling. The lead players, royalty of the underworld, were unknown to one another and scattered across all seven continents. The game's goal was to ignite the most chaos by committing crimes, inspiring mass debauchery, or exciting general entropy without being caught or having one's identity discovered. Either of those predicaments had the consequence of disqualification.

A panel of judges scored these acts; they were known collectively as The Figments. No soul had ever met or seen a Figment; nobody knew how many entities were involved with the group. As far as Petyr was concerned, the Figments didn't really need to exist. As long as he had a job, he could be working for a syndicate full of ghosts. The invisible judges were offering an incredible grand prize: the office of Hegemon of the known world. This blessing would be granted to the player who most quickly accrued one million chaos points. It was almost unbelievable. No players ever bothered to ask how the Figments would make it happen; the dream of such incredible power was more than enough motivation for most modern narcissists and new-age sociopaths.

The prize lured all types of players from all lots of life to the game. As such, all tactics and any deeds were fair game. Rape, treason, arson, murder, burglary, graffiti, and extortion were a few of the more common acts, but no limit was imposed on what was considered truly chaotic. In fact, the only written rules referred to the execution of the acts themselves.

Each player was required to announce his intent to commit a crime before the actual occurrence. This served to weed out the simple criminals from the true megalomaniac masterminds; crimes of passion were considered especially urbane. The nature of the entropic operation itself could remain a mystery, although bolder players might give some clues to their plans. These declarations acted as additional proof that the player was worthy of special credit for his chaotic conduct and often resulted in higher scores from the judges. It also gave other players an opportunity to stop the crime from happening and determine the player's identity. Given the devious nature of most prominent players, having one's identity discovered resulted in not only disqualification, but also an unfortunate demise.

At one time, Peter had been a Russian special agent; his training had prepared him well for the role he would play in the game. Disenfranchised from country and family, Petyr had abandoned his nation's secret service two years ago and sold his skills to an aristocratic game player claiming to be from Crete. He called himself the Minotaur, and he was slowly building an army of agents using a seemingly bottomless wallet to cover all expenses. Petyr was hired as a knight of chaos, committed to furthering the destruction of all orderly action. The Minotaur envisioned himself as some sort of destructive savior, claiming to have a grand manifesto, a great plan to reinvent the world after his ascension to the Hegemony. Petyr didn't care much for that aspect of Anonymous. As long as the gold was flowing into his coffers, his boss could pass an edict killing all puppies and stripping angels of their wings; the money was all that mattered.

Petyr continued waiting as the seconds drifted into minutes, melted into hours. The alarms he expected never sounded. Suddenly, the briefcase felt especially heavy. It only contained six syringes, snugly secured in foam bedding. Petyr was unsure as to the syringes' contents, but thought that a little ignorance was just fine. Not knowing every detail often made completing missions a lot simpler. This particular endeavor had already wound up being several levels more complicated than expected. The guards had been all too aware of his movements through the complex, despite his ingenious disguise and fleet feet; it was as though some third party had been setting the odds against him from the start.

Something felt amiss, as if the facility's air had been stagnant over thousands of years. Petyr briefly hallucinated that he was hiding in a tomb, trapped with his master pharaoh's treasure, six golden syringes of judgment. Shaking off the visions, Petyr convinced himself that whatever was in those needles wasn't worth dying over. He made a quick mental note: he wasn't getting paid nearly enough for this job. He would have to take it up with the Minotaur, if he could even escape. Though it wasn't specifically included in his orders, Petyr was determined to survive the day; dying was not his forte. He quickly decided that, if he was going to be forced to meet his maker, being slain while investigating the eerie calm was a much more appealing option than rotting in a corner.

Petyr took a deep breath and starting moving away from his safe alcove. He crept from shadow to shadow, retracing his steps back to the laboratory where he had found the vials. The facility was a complex, cold maze designed to trap research scientists for endless ages. Unable to find freedom, they would work hours upon hours to invent demented weapons and frivolous devices. Petyr had placed a timed explosive in the primary research lab, but he surmised that someone had found it and disarmed it. If the scientists had discovered it, then they might have been inferred that he hadn't been able to leave the premises.

Utmost stealth would be required for him to escape intact.

Petyr's muffled footsteps seemed to upset the heavy air, adding to the illusion that he was walking under a Great Pyramid. Something had unraveled his plan much worse than he had considered possible, as it often goes. A nasty tumor of worry knotted itself over and over in his stomach. He slowed his travel as he neared his destination, finally sidling up to the great, glass window-wall of the research department. Flourescent lights strobed erratically from the lab, casting arachnid shadows on the outer corridor wall. Petyr peered in, using his peak sneaking technique to avoid notice.

It wouldn't have mattered if he was carrying a bullhorn and singing Souza, there was no one left who could sing along. A scene of carnage flickered before his tired eyes. Scientists lay strewn throughout the room like litter, white lab coats stained red as robins. Great gashes lined many of the corpses' faces; often, the wounds were still leaking scarlet juices onto the floor. Petyr couldn't make out any facial features; the scientists' heads seemed to have gone through a mighty vise. Some vicious monster had violated this space, crushing all life beyond recognition. The flashing fluorescents illuminated two small sparkles on a stark laboratory bench. One was a silver tern, left by Petyr as an artist's signature after he stole the vials.

Petyr squinted, trying to gleam what the other sparkling speck might be.

He couldn't think fast enough; a pair of strong hands lifted him up and threw him through the laboratory window. His body turned to putty and his skin split from the force of the impact. Shards of glass cut him in hundreds of places, creating a jagged, ruby grid all along his torso; blood began to flow freely. Time began to slow as Petyr gliding through the air; he imagined himself looking like the mutilated scientists, an unidentifiable pulpy mass of flesh. Sliding along the ground in a puddle of mixed, crimson fluids, his mind spun, his heart raced, and he tried of think of a survival plan. His body crashed into the wall with a heavy thud. Peter couldn't lift his head or his fists; something vital had ruptured inside him. Heavy footsteps padded to his side. Two great hamfists pried the briefcase out of Petyr's petrified grip. As his fingers loosened, his mind began to fade into black.

A deep voice echoed through his fracturing mind. "Thank ya for helping the Hippo, sah. If ya wake up tomorrow, tell the Minotaur that the Epitaph send his regards."

Bifurcate

Train rides are always exceptionally boring, Dr. Hadjaz thought to himself, fighting hard to stay awake. He couldn't quite bring himself to trust the man sitting across from him, his supposed partner in crime. They had both been hired by the same mysterious stranger, The Epitaph, but that bond was of little worth. After all, they had both been chosen because they were the most ruthless artisans in their respective fields.

Dr. Hadjaz's traveling companion called himself the Dancing Hippo, and rightly so. The man was a true behemoth, a rippling monolith of a henchman. He looked as though he could eat literally eat a horse in one sitting. Dr. Hadjaz wasn't sure about where the "Dancing" title came from and didn't really care to know any details. The Hippo claimed he was wanted for murder in over one hundred countries, but Dr. Hadjaz wouldn't believe him before he did a thorough background check and had some serious data points. Even if that rumor weren't true, Dr. Hadjaz would have bet his first-descended testicle that it would be a terrible idea to cross The Hippo.

Their cabin was suited for four passengers, fitted with a pair of red, velvet-lined loveseats across from each other. The Hippo filled both seats on his side easily, with no room to spare. Despite being so monstrous, the henchman was dressed well in a white button up shirt and brown dress slacks. His tiny green bow-tie, speckled with white polka-dots, seemed intentionally ironic, but Hadjaz didn't dare ask. The Hippo had combed his hair immaculately, gelling it in place with obsessive design and far too much fixative.

None of this really bothered Dr. Hadjaz; he'd worked with too many kinds of low-life to be put off so easily. He had led a vigorous, noble life of medicinal research until a few years ago, when he realized that his time was slipping away and he was yet utterly unfulfilled. So, he decided to play Anonymous, signing up as The Good Doctor. The opportunities for research offered by playing the game were much more satisfying than the offerings of academic pursuit. The Doctor had worked for a few low-level players before realizing just how high his powerful brain could fly. As his ambitions grew greater and greater, he left the organizations of his employers in flaming rubble and flew like a phoenix ascending. This current assignment with the Epitaph was his greatest achievement yet, though he was certain things would only get better. To protect his identity, he designed himself an insignia, a purple winged man, representing his love of the Daedalus and Icarus. Though his everyday life flirted with danger, Dr. Hadjaz used cold logic to make sure he never flew too close to the sun.

No, Dr. Hadjaz had spent too much time in the heart of the game to be bothered by the Hippo's odd appearance and demeanor. What really dug at The Good Doctor was the silver briefcase. The Hippo held it tightly between his great hamfists, refusing even to store it in the luggage compartment. "The Hippo's only letting go of this to The Epitaph his-self." His commitment to completing his mission was admirable, if incredibly simple-minded.

Dr. Hadjaz had been hired specifically to examine whatever was inside the briefcase and he had no idea what it might contain. It could be a code for some ancient fortress, a weapon to melt the thickest armor, an elixir of immortality, or any number of other things. The Epitaph had given no clues, claiming only that it was "extremely entropic." The Good Doctor tried to think of other things. He dreamed of women he had known, of projects he had completed, and of lands he had traveled, but the briefcase kept sneaking in at the edge of his thoughts. Hadjaz began to grow tipsy with anticipation; he was not a doctor known for his patience.

Before devoting his life to the game, Dr. Hadjaz had run several labs. He had hired grad students and other research technicians to perform his research; he was usually too busy brainstorming his next project to do any experimentation himself. If an assignment wasn't yielding results within a few days, he claimed his staff was moving too slowly and the scheme was scrapped. He would replace all his scientists and start again on a new project. Luckily for his academic career, his strongest asset was creativity, so he had no shortage of alternate schemes to investigate. However, all his plots drove towards one ultimate goal, the betterment of mankind. The Good Doctor cringed to remember such a sterile existence; his life as a criminal genius was infinitely more intoxicating.

There are too many hours left in the train ride, Dr. Hadjaz started to shift anxiously in his seat. Not knowing what was in the briefcase, not being able to plan, expand, and extrapolate, and not getting his way was driving him stir crazy. His brain was on fire! He needed to initiate a plan to get his hands on that briefcase. He leaned forward, put his hands on his knees and stared directly at his associate.

"So, my dear partner, Mr. Hippo, are you ready to let me have a peek into that case yet?"

The Hippo didn't bother to look back at Dr. Hadjaz. "The Hippo already told ya, you're not going to get a look. The Hippo's only going to give it to the Epitaph. Stop asking before ya get The Hippo upset, sah."

"Now, listen to me," Dr. Hadjaz said, getting quickly annoyed, "We're supposed to work together, and it is my job to work with whatever is in that case. You must give it to me immediately!"

"Do ya think The Hippo cares? The Hippo only answers to the boss. The Epitaph is the boss, not ya, sah."

The Good Doctor rolled his eyes and sputtered a sigh through his tight lips. Extreme loyalty, tremendous strength, and simpleton intelligence. All these things made the Dancing Hippo a perfect henchman; they also made him an intolerable partner.

The Hippo had searched The Doctor before allowing him onto the train, on the Epitaph's orders. However, he had only been ordered to search for weapons, which Hadjaz did not usually carry. He packed a much more dangerous variety of items of his own invention. He pulled a pen out of his jacket pocket and began to nibble on its end.

"Hmm. You see, that attitude is going to be quite a problem. If we're going to get along, we need to trust one another, right? I don't feel very much trust in this cabin."

The Hippo refused to reply; he simply stared at the bit of air directly behind the Dr. Hadjaz's left earlobe.

The Good Doctor smiled impishly. If that was how it was going to be, then he could play along. Dr. Hadjaz didn't like to put his cards down before it was absolutely necessary, but the situation was driving him up the wall. He took the pen from his mouth and stuck his arm out towards the Hippo. He closed his eyes and clicked the pen's button three times. A light at the tip of the pen emitted a flash of green light, rapidly followed by flashes of pink light and green light in a highly complex pattern.

"Good Hippo," Dr. Hadjaz commanded, "You will give me that briefcase and you will be happy about it. You will work with me from now on, instead of against me. It is in your best interests to do so. For all intents and purposes, I am your boss now. Got it?"

The Hippo's expression hadn't changed. His typically serene face looked exactly the same. Dr. Hadjaz was worried; his brow twitched and leaked tiny beads of sweat. Had something gone wrong? Was this massive monster immune to his hypnosis device?

The Hippo extended his arm, briefcase still attached, to the middle of the cabin. "Yes, sah, The Hippo obeys." He dropped the case onto the floor.

The Good Doctor smiled a genuine smile, like a child on his birthday, and quickly scrambled to pick up his treasure. "Thank you very much, dear friend. I think we'll be getting along just fine from now on."

He opened the case while short of breath; his heart beat quickly, pitter-pattering with excitement. Inside the case he found six syringes, all containing an unknown clear liquid, all labeled BioMod36B. The vials piqued the scientist's interest; his

Faustian soul was yearning for knowledge about this strange solution. An insatiable urge to explore the serum's magic filled his very fibers. In a day or two, he would have a lab to himself where he could experiment to his heart's content. On the other hand, he had a willing test subject sitting across from him.

"Hey there, Hippo. To celebrate our new friendship, I have a little game to play. Are you interested?"

"Yes, sah. The Hippo likes all sorts of games, but especially chess."

"Ah, well. Very good then. This is going to be just like chess. Just sit tight and close your eyes, alright?"

The Doctor took one of the syringes and checked it for bubbles. There was no use killing off his patient before he got his data. After he was satisfied the injectible was safe, the Doctor walked over to the Hippo and placed the point of the needle against the Hippo's neck.

"Bon voyage." Dr. Hadjaz inserted the needle into the Hippo's jugular and pressed on the plunger until the entire contents had been administered. Dancing Hippo sat through the process with little more and an uncomfortable grunt. Dr. Hadjaz wasn't concerned about the dosage; his patient was big enough to require a whole flask of cough syrup to see any effect.

The Doctor returned to his seat to watch his experiment in motion. Nothing happened for several minutes; the Hippo blankly stared at that same sector of empty air he loved so well. After about a quarter of an hour had passed, the Hippo silently conked out.

Perhaps the dosage had been too great after all? Maybe the specimen was dead! The Good Doctor panicked for a second-and-a-half; the Epitaph would surely be upset that he'd killed a fine henchman. He quickly shook off the worry and began to think rationally. The Doctor didn't believe the serum was just meant for killing a foe or for making someone pass out; there was too little chaos involved in either act, though they were both quite villainous. Even so, one vial might have been too much for the Hippo to handle.

Just as Dr. Hadjaz was making a mental note of the failed experiment, the Hippo sat straight up, stiff as a board. His eyes were bestially wild, entirely opposite from their usual tranquil-pool state. A strand of drool began to run out the corner of his mouth; his whole body was quaking rapidly, as if he were being electrocuted. He shuddered and quivered and made quite a racket. He whooped and hollered, shouting out sounds only vaguely reminiscent of words. A small, spherical growth appeared on his neck, at the point where he'd been injected with the serum. It grew rapidly, inflating like a fleshy water balloon. When it was the size of a tennis ball, the tumor detached from its host and bounced to the center of the cabin; the Hippo passed out once more.

Dr. Hadjaz stared at the small lump of flesh with terrified eyes, fascination locking his vision in place. This was unfamiliar territory for the scientist; he was witnessing a miracle of sorts, something that didn't make sense. Things were happening before him that bent the laws of science in ways he had not imagined possible. The ball of cells continued to grow, changing shape as it expanded. It slowly morphed its shape, taking on the features of a small child. After a half an hour, it looked like a young man, distinctly overweight. As it continued to expand and mature it looked more and more like the Hippo asleep behind it.

A bifurcation serum! Dr. Hadjaz couldn't believe it. It was a serum that could replicate the test subject. It seemed unreal. He closed his eyes and shook his head, planning to wake up from a mad dream. He though this must be the product of some long-dormant dementia. When he opened his eyes it confirmed that he was living in a nightmare. The cloned Hippo was prodding the original, trying to wake him up. The original begrudgingly regained consciousness and was surprisingly calm about what he saw.

"Hello, The Hippo," said the newborn clone, "Are ya feeling all right?"

"Oh yes, The Hippo," spoke the original doppelganger. "The Hippo was just napping! The Hippo feels much better now."

Dr. Hadjaz was contemplating jumping out the cabin window when a wayward fist rapped at the door. Hippo Number Two opened it to reveal the train car's attendant. The stiff young man pushed a pair of thick-rimmed glasses further up his nose before trying to speak.

"I'm sorry to bother you but I heard a commotion. Um, weren't there only the two of you before? Hey! Are you trying to scam us?" He took a noble stance and puffed up his chest. "I'm sorry, I'm going to have to alert my boss."

The two Hippos shared a quick glance before grabbing the attendant's arms and pulling him into the cabin.

"No, sah. That won't be necessary."

They picked the boy up and swung him as hard as they could through the cabin window. The attendant disappeared with a crash and a scream, and Dr. Hadjaz decided he was glad he hadn't gone through the window; the train was moving quite rapidly, after all. The cabin was stiflingly silent for several moments afterward; the only sound came from wind whistling through the broken window.

The new Hippo put his finger to his lips, wrinkling in his chubby brow to indicate deep thought. The Good Doctor realized that this clone wasn't under his hypnotic spell and it worried him. The air in his mouth turned exceptionally dry.

"Hmm," the doctor said, laughing nervously, "There isn't enough room in here for all us, is there?"

Dr. Hadjaz spent the rest of the train ride nestled in the lap of Hippo Number Two, wishing that he could be back in his old university lab, performing research on the mundane and uninteresting.

Cunnilingus

As he regained consciousness, Petyr briefly thought that he had died and gone to heaven. Despite his years of atheistic fervor, he had managed to arrive at nirvana. His vision was swirling with images of beautiful women, all beckoning him nearer with sparkling, doe eyes. His own eyes had turned into kaleidoscopes; repeating images of the women spiraled into the distance, as far as he could see. He gathered his strength and tried to skip toward the gorgeous females, but his arms were yanked back before he could finish his first hop.

That harsh jerk forced dreamy visions to fade into a much harsher reality. Cold, metal shackles adorned Petyr's wrists, securely attaching him to sturdy rings in the stone wall behind him; the rings were located at shoulder height, trapping his arms perpendicular to his body. A sharp pain pierced his senses like an infant on an airplane, its epicenter on his breast. He looked down to see two metal clamps, one attached to each nipple; the clamps were also equipped with wires running up into the ceiling above him.

The infinite fractal of spiraling beauty began to settle down; thousands of sultry faces congealed onto one seductive body. Petyr recognized the figure of his captor immediately; her silhouette informed him that his notion of a heavenly future couldn't be further from his present situation.

The tall, scathingly clothed woman stepped closer to her captive, shifting her hips like a horse in heat. She was wearing a red leather one-piece that stopped short, halfway down her thighs; the neckline dipped low, almost down to her waistline, exposing ample cleavage. Her bosom might have fallen out, but six small buckles, evenly spaced, attached the sides of the swooping neckline. Black combat boots with four-inch heels gave her an exceedingly overwhelming, but undeserved air of authority.

"Dear god or whoever," Petyr mumbled, "Why couldn't you have just let me die?"

"Vell, vell, look who has voken up. Is naptime over, my little raccoon dog? Are you ready to play vith me?"

Petyr sighed and spoke, his voice monotonous like a lonely robot. "No, mistress. I'm not in a playful mood today. I'm glad to see you're still keeping things business casual."

The Dom Com, sometimes called the Himalayan Minx, unveiled a wide, sharp grin. She had finally caught her prized quarry after months of failed attempts. Little was known about the voluptuous mercenary, other than her penchant for wearing leather, her Eurasian origin, and her extremely sadistic tendencies. A prominent Anonymous player known as the Bullmoose had hired her as an assassin, but the Dom Com's objective in Anonymous was not to help him win the game. Instead, her goal was to force others to lose. Nothing ignited her pleasure center like breaking an opponent's will, cracking them like a raw egg and sucking out the insides. If she were in an especially good mood, there would be beating and whipping of the eggs. The Dom Com used an encyclopedic knowledge of torture techniques to interrogate her captives. After her violent thirst was quenched, she would force her prisoners to reveal their names and disqualify them from the game. Her tactics were quick and dirty, much like the woman herself. She and Petyr had a special relationship; he was certain that she had special treats waiting to surprise him.

"Can we just get this started aleady?" Petyr asked. "I've got an appointment with my dentist tomorrow. I'm pretty excited about this root canal we've got planned."

"Oh, silly boy, ve can call him up and reschedule," the Dom Com said, tying her hair up in a short bun. "I've been vaiting so long to catch up vith you! I'm sure you've got a lot to tell me."

The Dom Com had been tracking Petyr for over nine months. They had first met on assignment, their missions at odds with one another. Petyr had been sent by the Minotaur to capture a genetically-engineered, super chimpanzee from a research facility; the Com had been sent to erase it. Petyr managed to sneak the ape away safely by disguising it as a janitor. From that day forth, the sultry assassin had sworn to achieve vengeance. Every month or so, they would find themselves at odds once more and again Petyr would use his superior tactics to outmaneuver her. She never surrendered, and her day for revenge had come at last.

Petyr winced. He must have been unconscious a long while for her to catch him so easily. That meant the briefcase, the mission, and his life, were all forfeit. His embarrassment must have shown all over his face, because the Dom Com walked over and pinched his cheeks into a smile.

"No, no. Ve can't have you being so unhappy. You have such a pretty face. Look, I vant you to meet somebody. It's somebody I think you'll like." She stepped back and clapped her hands aggressively. "Aleister! Attend!"

A door creaked open behind the Dom Com and a portly caucasian man scuttled into the room. He was wearing nothing more than a black latex speedo and a matching collar, revealing a flabby torso spattered with coarse, graying hair; the shambling man looked like the love-child of a grizzly bear and a manatee. He shuffled over to his mistress holding a heavy bucket, eyes focused on its turbulent contents.

31

"This playtoy, he is new since ve last met. My little fox, are you familiar vith the Snapdragon? You know his vork?"

"Sure, he's one of the best henchmen around. He's supposedly released hundreds of convicted murderers from high security compounds and never even had a photo taken. Quite the impressive record."

"Yes, he is a player, just like you. That is, he was, until I learned his name. Please, I vant you to meet Aleister Bowfinger, once known as the Snapdragon. Now, after being shamefully diskvalified, he became my slave. Much better than the typical alternative, yes?" She raised an eyebrow, hoping her prey would be duly impressed, or at least a little intimidated.

Petyr was neither. "I don't know. Probably. Maybe? What did you do with my briefcase? Where are the samples?"

The Dom Com paced over to her prisoner; her torso hovered perfectly still as her waist gyrated in a hypnotic orbit below it. "I don't know anything about that. I vas assigned a mission to kill some scientists. I come to this site and I find my vork completed! Vat a disappointment! However, I also found you vrapped up like a present from the heavens, so I am not too upset."

"You really don't know who you're messing with. The Minotaur will come after me and do terrible, embarrassing things to you and your boss," Petyr bluffed. He had no illusions about his employer; The Minotaur was much more likely to look for the briefcase and its contents than a dispensable agent, no matter how skilled that agent might be. "He will stop at nothing to get that briefcase and its secrets. Come on, what have you done with it?"

The Dom Com clicked her tongue discerningly. "I already told you, I don't know vhat you are talking about. Also, I don't think you quite understand the little role-play ve have going on. I am the one vith the pover right now." She reached into her boot and pulled out a small black cylinder with a big red button, a trigger for some unseen device. "I have some qvestions for you, my naughty pup. I hope you vill answer correctly, for your sake. Do you remember how ve first met?"

The clamps were siphoning too much blood to Petyr's nipples. He was certain they would fall off his chest. They were all too sure of the purpose behind the Dom's trigger. "Yes. It was in Jakarta. Nine moths ago, I think. I was there to escort a chimpanzee that somehow managed to discover a solution to some equation or other. Something about the energy shortage. You were there to kill the very same ape, to stop the chimp's brainpower from being used for good or something. I don't know. It was a mission; it's long done. I like to keep things simple."

The Dom Com politely clicked her button; a small shock coursed through the clamps, turning Petyr's veins to molten sludge. He knew the Dom meant it as little more than a warning; his situation would become much more excruciating over the next several hours.

"Not qvuite, you scamp. That vas the first time we met as cloak and dagger, but not the first time ve met as man and voman. Do you remember, two years ago, vhen you vere on leave in Moscow?"

This question took Petyr by surprise. To him, the trip to Moscow had just been another vacation, another opportunity for him to waste his money on pleasure and debauchery. He remembered the city and its offerings well, but nothing struck him as significant about his time there.

"I remember. I was on leave for almost a week. What about it?"

"You took my viginity from me!" the Dom Com screamed, pressing the button with vigor. "You stole it vith your mouth! In the bathroom at the Kremlin's Korner! How can you not remember this?"

As terrible jolts of electricity caused him to dissociate from his body, Petyr had a vision of his past. He remembered going to the Kremlin's Korner while he was in Moscow. The trouble was, he didn't remember leaving. It was the most popular bar in his hotel's district, known for serving a drink dubbed the Molotov Cocktail. The drink was simple; it consisted of a shot of vodka with high enough proof that it could be lit on fire. Petyr had lost count after swallowing around seven. His Russian blood had granted him immunity from cold weather, but had neglected an ability to tolerate alcohol. His liquor processing system was so weak that he didn't remember much of the next two days after that night of debauchery. He certainly couldn't recall a fun romp with anyone like the Dom Com. Deranged as she might be, Petyr would have treasured memories of a night with her.

"I'm sorry," Petyr said, panting, "I don't recall. Maybe you're confusing me with someone else. I was-"

Before he could finish, more intense shocks wracked his body. His spine arched, his wrists burned where they were attached to the metal rings. The Dom Com was through maintaining onto any pretense of playing nice.

"Don't mess vith me. Hah! As if I could forget your face. I stared into your eyes for a good...no, an amazing hour." She shivered, a wave of pleasure flooding her through the memory. Aleister straightened up his posture, hopeful that his skills might be required after all. "I recognized you immediately in Jakarta. Do you know, I have been vith no man since then? I had been vith no man before then. You are the only man for me, my little fox. I vill have you as my pet, forever."

Petyr was shocked, electrified, and silent; he was disgusted to think that he might have been responsible for creating such a sadistic monster.

"Now tell me, vat is your darkest secret?" As she yelled, the Dom Com pulled the torture trigger once more. All of Petyr's senses flared intensely as electricity overclocked his system; he experienced sensations unknown by most creatures limited to only five senses. Self-immolation couldn't hurt half as badly as what Petyr was experiencing, a transubstantiation into an electrical entity. He tasted metal, as if an unwashed sword were cutting out his tongue. Colors flashed before his eyes, constructing a tempered mosaic of his life's memories. A sweet siren's song twittered in his ear, tempting him to obey his new master, to give in to inertia's flow. As the shock died down, a hint of cinnamon lingered in his nostrils.

Petyr hung motionless and out of breath, a stressful euphoria replacing the unbearable torture; his body was entirely limp and useless. The only things keeping him upright were the chains on his wrists. He could see the excitement in his captor's eyes; she licked her lips and fondled the shock trigger like a lover.

Peter knew exactly how this farce would play out; his years of training had prepared him for situations just like this one. He could avoid telling the mistress anything, just as long as she could keep torturing him; his mind was locked in a steel vise and pain was not its key. And yet, from a distance, his body was telling him that those shocks hurt like hell. His future held endless days of pain with no respite in sight. The Dom Com would work him hard a couple of days, before seeing his resilient nature shine through. She would inevitably grow bored, and set up an automated torture regiment while she was otherwise occupied; this robotic painfest would continue until Petyr was dead or rescued.

Unfortunately, Petyr also knew what the Minotaur was planning. Failure of his mission left Petyr as good as dead in the Minotaur's eyes; his employer wouldn't be sending any rescue missions, limiting Petyr's futures to various forms of gruesome expiration. If Petyr managed to escape, he would no longer be welcome in the Minotaur's circle. He would be blacklisted to prevent him joining any other Anonymous syndicates and would probably run into more than a few hungry assassins. Most futures appeared pretty bleak for the shocked agent.

There was only one viable option available to Petyr; only one choice would allow him to stop the cycle before it could even begin. It might place him in an even more dangerous situation, but at least he would see a glimmer of hope that he might survive. As long as he survived, he could find another source of money. He could find another reason for living. He looked directly at the Dom Com, his blue eyes colder than the Russian steppes.

"Mistress Com, my name is Petyr Dmitriev."

Dirge

"I hereby call this emergency meeting, the Two Hundred Thirty-First Congress of Figments, to Session. Please be seated."

Coelocanth, the Figment of Order, remained standing while his congregation took their seats; his deep voice reverberated through the narrow hall. Coelocanth was the eldest of the Figments, the first to manifest in this world. He had followed the scriptures of Chaos since long before any of the other Figments were even conceived.

The tall, snow-bearded man sent a solemn gaze to each of his companions. These six dedicated souls, his younger family members, sat around a circular, stone table at the heart of Castle Figment. One chair remained empty; it waited for the day its Master would manifest to sit upon it.

"We must begin at once, we have so much to discuss," Coelacanth continued. "As you are no doubt well aware, our game Anonymous is approaching its final stages; several players are close to achieving one million points. The level of chaos on the planet is higher than it has ever been before. While this news should bring us all glad tidings, there have been some complications, some kinks in our grand scheme. I have asked Archimedes to explain his discoveries to you."

Archimedes stood rapidly, his wiry frame uncoiling from a cramped seating position. His body was long and skinny, full of angles nearly as sharp as his mind. The Logic Figment constantly kept a terse frown dancing on his thin lips.

"Welcome, family. Ahem! I wish our gathering could happen under more joyous circumstances. Unfortunately, I bring you both good news and bad news. Ahem. Allow me to start with the bad news.

"The velocity of entropy generation in the world has slowed down to almost zero points per day. Randomness has reached a plateau, and it is unclear how long this situation will last. Ahem! In other words, in the current situation it is unlikely we will reach the critical level of chaos required to release our master from his trans-dimensional bondage."

This news incited a roar of disappointment from the other Figments.

"What do you mean by this?" The table shook and rattled as Valkyrie, Violence Figment, slammed her fists against the stone surface. Her face was a freckled mask of wrath, from snarling lips to wrinkled brow. Her hair was braided in thick pigtails that dangled down below her broad shoulders; the braids carried an electric charge, diffusing anger from her core to the standing air around her. Terra and Archimedes, the Figments sitting closest to the raging fury, backed away cautiously.

"Everything we have done and worked for, it was all for naught?" Valkyrie fumed. "Unacceptable! Unforgivable! Explain this, scientist. Try to appease me with your tedious logic! Tell us who is responsible and I'll go pummel them to sleep!"

"Ahem! Thank you, everyone," Archimedes said, "For allowing me finish my statements and continue onto the good news. I recalibrated one of the entropometers, effectively rendering it an anti-entropometer. With it, I am able to monitor the flow of order in the universe instead of the flow of chaos. Simple logic, really. I'm amazed I'd never thought of it before. Ahem! It appears that a growing number of entities are opposing the entropy we create. The velocity of order has nearly approached the same level as chaos.

"The way things are now, it appears we are accelerating toward a more ordered universe. If we don't act quickly, the velocity of randomness generation in the universe will become negative. Reality will begin to reverse our hard work and start heading toward a destiny filled by utter organization; this is unbearably far from the goal we have set four ourselves. I mean, that our Master has set for us."

40

"But isn't that just how it goes?" Oedipus, the Irony Figment, felt obligated to propose an alternative opinion whenever possible. Rather than sitting, she was perched upside down in her seat, performing a headstand with her hands on the chair's arms. She was wearing a black-and-white striped, strapless dress; both her breasts and her hemline ignored the effects of gravity. "The natural order is to return to a mean state, right? We couldn't make the world chaotic enough, fast enough, and now we've missed our window because Nature is balancing things out. Isn't that a simple explanation what is happening? It was inevitable. Deal with it."

"I'm sorry sister, but I must beg to differ with your opinion. The natural trend is certainly towards chaos. I should know." Terra, the Wilding Figment felt he was the definitive expert on what was natural. Terra refused to deal with artificial constructs unless absolutely necessary, clothing and bathing both falling under his definition of necessary. "Archimedes, this trend that you've observed is certainly artificial. There must be some sort of disgusting, unnatural force working against us. I wish I could spit all over it."

Lazarus, the Chronicle Figment, placed one finger on the table. "Quit wasting our time, you ignorant tits. I'm going to stop this squabble before it starts. I can see it's going to get us nowhere. I am the Chronicle Figment, after all." Lazarus paused for a moment, to allow his awesomeness room to breathe. "You are both right, in a sense. Oedipus, the machinations of the universe do dictate a return to the median state. Terra, the force behind this negative acceleration is supernatural."

"You know how much I hate it when you use that word," Terra mumbled.

Ignoring his younger brother, Lazarus continued. "However, you are both fundamentally wrong in your assumptions. That makes sense, I suppose. A man of my abilities must have foresight as strong as his hindsight. Allow me to clarify for you, baby siblings.

"I can see that we are dealing with something entirely different from what we are prepared to encounter. We are entering unfamiliar territory." Lazarus was the least favorite sibling of the Figments. Though he was blessed with the gift of oracle, he kept details of his prophecies to himself. There were only rare occasions when he would divulge his visions, instances when he could flaunt his power and reveal much he knew about the future. The other Figments all agreed: he was a king among asses. "I had a vision the other day-"

"AHEM!" Archimedes cleared his throat with exceptional vigor, like a cannon booming over open seas. "I haven't been able to finish what I have been needing to say, thank you." He was beginning to get flustered. "I haven't given you the worst news, yet."

Oedipus rolled her eyes and muttered under her breath. "You mentioned good news and bad news, not worst news, nerd."

The scientist ignored her remark and revealed his tidings. "The agents responsible for this unbearable turn of events are human."

Another fervorous din rose among the Figments.

"I knew you were going to say that," Lazarus shouted. "But I didn't want to believe it."

Valkyrie was up in arms, out of her seat with fists raised at the ceiling. "Don't fuck around! That's impossible! Are you trying to tell me that the mortals have discovered a means to compete with our might? Coelacanth, end this meeting right this second. Give me the word and I'll go crush those wimpy ants right away."

Oedipus rolled her eyes. "You can't seriously believe they're responsible for this sudden surge of order. There has got to be another more reasonable explanation. Like, maybe there's a bizzarro group just like us somewhere on earth. What if they're disseminating order instead of chaos? Wouldn't that be something?" The Irony Figment chuckled.

Valkyrie flashed a sneer back at Oedipus, but didn't say anything.

Coelocanth frowned through his salty beard. "Are you absolutely certain? There is no chance of error in your measurements?"

Archimedes nodded. "Yes. I'm very sure. Ahem. I suppose it is possible that some human scientists got a hold of some of our entropic emitters and reverse engineered them. I mean, I could do it in a few minutes. If they'd discovered one a few centuries ago, maybe they could have discovered a method to reverse the polarities and cancel the effects by now."

"Who cares about why it's happening? Let's do something to fix it!" Valkyrie's temper flared again; her mood was especially turbulent. "I've been itching to try out some of the techniques I've been inventing. Let's go slaughter those mortal bastards right now!"

Terra refuted his sister's notion. "Come now, we've gone so long without influencing them directly. Let's just ride this wave of organization out; it's surely just a temporary fix. Once these meddling humans die, the flow of chaos will return to normal. We'll still be around, ruining the organization they love so much. Just be patient, sis."

"I don't think so!" Valkyrie spat, "You're just a lazy, dirty bum, Terra. You aren't nearly wild enough for your own good! How are those idiot humans going to learn anything if we don't teach them with our fists!"

A debate raged for half an hour before family strife reached a tipping point.

"Silence, children!" Coelocanth boomed, his commanding aura whipping through the room. The intensity in the air cooled instantly from a violent boil to a low simmer. "You all know the rules as well as I do. We cannot influence the inhabitants of Earth directly, with our abilities. Our Master forbade us from touching human lives until he joins us here. I cannot risk any of you upsetting him, before he graces us with his presence. We are doing everything for him! Do not forget that!"

The other Figments glanced awkwardly around the table as their elder continued to speak. "I have taken measures to prevent any overzealous activities. The Threshold is sealed. There will be no more travel between Figment Island and Earth until our Master is among us. The mechanisms of Anonymous are in place, blessed by our Lord. As soon as the game is won, an explosive maniac will become Hegemon. He will take the reins of human destiny into his unstable hands and cause plenty of entropy. We must have faith in our Lord's design, that His plan will lead Earth into unfathomable chaos. Do you understand the significance of the situation?"

Begrudging acquiescence leaked out, across the table. The siblings understood well. Despite their silly quarrels, they had one thing in common; each of them wanted to please their Master, their common Father. A vibrant shame turned the air of the congressional chamber to gelatinous gas.

"Well, come on," Oedipus blurted at Archimedes, who sat mumbling to himself, maddened by guilt. "Give us that good news you promised. Something has got to compensate for this disaster."

Archimedes looked perplexed. "Oh, did I mention that? Ahem. Well, yes, I suppose I'd forgotten. I'm not actually the one who is going to speak the good words. Ahem. Are you ready to speak for us?"

One Figment had remained silent throughout the entire family quarrel. Ophelia, the Psyche Figment, had sat unperturbed as her peers argued ineffectively over different plans of action. Because she was the youngest of the Figments, only a few years into the world, Ophelia had a special connection with her Father that the others had lost over time. She was an inter-dimensional ansible.

"I have received another important message from our Lord and Master," she rasped. The jagged red lightning in her eyes and her dearth of energy was proof that she had not slept much in the last several weeks. Communications were coming more frequently than ever before and were impossible to ignore. Recently, her head had been filled with a constant drone of her Master's thoughts and instructions.

"Come on, then. Spit it out! What did he say? Tell us!" Valkyrie waited on no man or woman to get what she wanted.

Ophelia nodded exhaustedly. "It's easier if I recreate the scene. I can't actually remember what happened too clearly. Give me a moment." She stood up from her chair, lowered her head, and dangled her arms at her sides, palms out. She held that position for several minutes, her siblings' eyes focused intently on the top of her head.

Suddenly, Ophelia's head jerked upright and she unleashed an ethereal scream. It was the kind of scream that could hunt its prey for miles and pierce their eardrums. It was a living breathing entity of its own rite, birthed from demonic sacrifice on a perpendicular plane. All of the Figments, even Valkyrie, jumped in their chairs, backing away from the terrifying woman before them. This was no longer their sister, but a holy icon of their Lord. Only Coelacanth seemed unfazed, eagerly awaiting this new message from his Father and only friend. Slowly, the scream winnowed down to a calmer tone. Ophelia's continued to channel her conversation, singing lyrics to a tuneless melody:

Devout servants, My Brothers and Sisters, My time is nearly nigh. The scales of fate are tipped in My favor. I am crowning from the womb of your efforts but I know there have been complications.

The reality you inhabit is not fully prepared for My presence, too much Order yet remains. Do not quail, My kin, My loves. Have faith and wait for the day of My arrival. I portend that We shall be reunited within a galactic heartbeat's time.

Do not forget, I bring such powerful change that the world as We know it shall cease to exist. In its stead, We will build a world of our own devising. I, Midas the Creation Figment, promise you that.

Go forth, sweet vassals, emissaries of My will, and sing My praise: a dirge of birth and rebirth, eternally repeating.

Entrenched

After their train ride, the misanthropic trio of Doctor, Hippo, and Hippo took a banana-colored cab to their final destination, a gunmetal skyscraper that disappeared into the sky, its top floor far beyond the cloud line. In the lobby, a dark haired receptionist with tight features led them to an elevator that was supposed to carry them down to their quarters. Dr. Hadjaz thought the idea of underground quarters was strange, but didn't mention anything to his companions. They weren't the type to exchange words, built like boulders and just as silent. The Good Doctor soon realized that the tall edifice launched into the sky was just a show for simple-minded passers-by.

Once it had descended a few hundred yards, the lift opened and its inhabitants spilled out into a large, cavernous amphitheater. A fifty-yard movie screen was hung like a portal above sprawling stage. At least thirty rows of black pleather chairs were tiered such that there was not a bad seat in the house. The "house" was more like a bunker; a whole regiment could have sat comfortably in the available seats. Less than a minute after the trio's arrival, a video began to play, projected from some invisible source. Trumpets blared a heroic fanfare as the lights dimmed and the secretary ushered her wards to their seats.

A deep, excited voice filled the air; it sounded like it belonged to a radio jockey, intensely aroused by the next song he was going to play. "Welcome, friends, to Epitaph Industries! Congratulations on your new positions!" The screen was filled with cartoons of smiling children, dancing dogs, and expensive houses. The children were merrily dancing and singing some gibberish lyrics while the dogs wagged their tails politely. "Here at EI, we only accept the most qualified candidates for careers under our roof. That's right, I'm talking about you! You're the best people to help us reach the stars and make our dreams reality! Always remember, our goals are the people's goals, and the people's goal is freedom. Freedom to be born the way they want, to live the way they want, and to die the way they want."

Suddenly, the horny fanfares screeched to a halt. The children on the screen stopped singing and looked upwards at some distraction yet invisible to the audience. Their faces were masks of fear, stuck the way their mothers always teased them they might freeze. "There are forces at play that want to end this way of life, our sacred right as human beings!" A giant globe fell from the sky, sending the children into a tizzy as they tried to escape; the dogs went mad, snapping at each other and all the children, non-discriminately. More than a few tykes and pups were crushed as the great sphere bounced around the screen, homing in on anything that moved. The globe bore the emblem from the Hegemon's family crest.

Very subtle, Dr. Hadjaz thought. He glanced over at his companions. The Hippos stared blankly at the movie with content smiles on their mirrored faces, unfazed by the strangeness of the situation. They seemed to think this screening to be a very agreeable welcoming party.

The video continued for several more minutes like a fugue, emphatically repeating its theme. The screen showed a variety of scenes, all involving happy people and their animal friends. Every scene portrayed some utopian ideal being destroyed; things looked idyllic for a moment, but the bouncing Hegemon ball would stop by and ruin everything for everybody. Meanwhile, the announcer's voice babbled on about the noble aspirations of Epitaph Industries and how, through their valiant efforts, they would change the world to a better place, where free will was truly free for every person. There was no mention of the game Anonymous, no mention of the grand prize, and no mention of the lives that would be destroyed as a result of the EI's actions.

Dr. Hadjaz couldn't help but notice the similarities between this video and one of the old conscription propaganda tapes. In the era just before the formation of the Hegemony, when humanity was on the brink of destroying itself, these types of videos were very common. They were used to promote patriotism and instill hope in countries razed by weapons and soiled by plagues, a last ditch effort to revitalize comatose societies.

Lots of bright colors and noises distracted from the real meaning behind the film: welcome to the war party, don't forget to check your hat.

After a hapless poodle was rolled into a pancake, the video drew to a close but the announcer would not let his audience leave quite yet. "Please stay seated for a word from your employer!"

In silence, on a white background, bold, black words of the Epitaph appeared on the screen:

WELCOME. I AM SURE YOU UNDERSTAND WHY YOU WERE EACH CHOSEN TO PLAY THIS GAME. I DON'T NEED TO HOLD YOUR HANDS. THIS INITIATION CEREMONY WAS JUST A FORMALITY FOR LESSER HENCHMEN. MINIONS OF COMMON CALIBER.

JUST GET BUSY AND CREATE SOME CHAOS. I WILL SEND YOU MISSIONS PERIODICALLY, BUT FOR NOW JUST KEEP ON DOING WHAT YOU DO BEST. WHEN I RELIEVE THE HEGEMON OF HIS DUTIES, YOUR REWARDS WILL BE MERIT BASED.

ALSO, HIPPOS, JUST GIVE THE SCIENTIST A CHANCE FOR ME. HE'S A NERD, FOR CRYING OUT LOUD.

It wasn't long before Dr. Hadjaz realized his instincts were correct; he was entrenched in a war where his knowledge was the most powerful weapon.

Two weeks into their habitation in the underground lair, Dr. Hadjaz and the Hippos still hadn't met with the Epitaph, face to face. The Doctor surmised that they never would. The Epitaph only communicated through typed messages; he was achingly careful not to give away any trace of his identity. He managed all his employees by sending orders at the beginning of each day. At the end of the day, he would release a report on how much chaos had been generated by Epitaph Industries and how much overtime would have to be worked over the weekend. Because he was a high-clearance employee, Dr. Hadjaz also received reports about the attacks on EI outposts in other countries. The other Anonymous players would stop at nothing to win.

The Doctor hadn't realized the extent to which Epitaph Industries permeated the world. It had nearly one two million total employees causing chaos throughout the globe. No part of the Hegemony was left untouched by EI. No depth of ocean was left unsplashed, no dark crevasse unspelunked. If it weren't spread so thinly with so many enemies, the corporation could have easily declared itself a sovereign nation.

Despite his aloofness, the Epitaph turned out to be a very generous employer. Dr. Hadjaz's location, the EI Eastern European headquarters, was equipped with a complete laboratory, outfitted with the most advanced instruments for every test imaginable and then some. He also provided a near limitless expense account, in case anything unforeseen was required, for any reason. Everything was just as Dr. Hadjaz had hoped it would be; he had found an elysian neighborhood, just like the children from the initiation videos. However, though The Good Doctor was given free reign to experiment as he liked, the Epitaph had very specific needs for the immediate future.

The Doctor's first objectives were to analyze the bifurcation serum, replicate it, and, ultimately, find an extremely chaotic use for it.

The first task yielded surprising results, almost immediately. The liquid in the syringe was less a serum and more an automated modeling kit. It was comprised of complex nanomachines and a superdense blend of common biological molecules and stem cells. The nanobots were programmed to take a reading of the subject's DNA, estimate his age from genetic decay, and using that data, sculpt a clone from the superdense material. It was a simple concept to create a complex organism; the Doctor wouldn't have believed it worked, but he'd seen it do magic before his own eyes.

Once Dr. Hadjaz had extracted the code from the nanobots, it took him only three days to completely recreate the serum. An extreme anal-retentive, by this time the Doctor had already optimized his daily work schedule. He allotted one hour sleeping at midnight, spent the next ten hours working, slept one hour at noon, and used his remaining ten hours to work through the night. He reserved one hour for leisure time during each work cycles immediately before his rest time; he realized the importance of diverting his attention to other tasks so that his subconscious could work on solving problems, too.

Improving the serum proved to be a trickier task that he had anticipated. The code inside the nanomachines proved to be incredibly intricate; Dr. Hadjaz realized it would be extremely tedious to try and get a good understanding of their basic functions before experimentation. Tedium wasn't his area of expertise; he preferred a blind shotgun analysis. A few test injections of modified code were horrible disasters. In his first batch of test subjects, one monkey was duplicated with a second head right above his buttocks; another duplication resulted in siamese triplets, forming a triangle walled by their merged arms.

Almost all the functions in the code used recursion to call on other functions, so changing a single variable or constant would result in drastic changes of output. He wanted to ask other scientists for advice, but they were too absorbed in their own research to care.

Self-important bastards! Dr. Hadjaz thought. *Your research is hardly as vital as mine! Ha! It's not like you'd have been able to solve my problems anyway.*

Dr. Hadjaz's silent, gargantuan partners weren't particularly helpful either. In fact, they were often more frustrating than his academic colleagues. The Doctor's hypnosis technique had long since worn off and the device couldn't be used on the same victim a second time. That victim would more than likely punch the Doctor in the neck before he could flip the switch. The Hippo Twins would only take orders directly from the Epitaph himself; the Doctor couldn't ask them to do anything himself unless he could get the Epitaph's approval to back him. Nor could he ask them for advice in his research because they were simpletons, at best.

The Hippos were inseparable. Either all of their missions were two man jobs or the Epitaph was a huge fan of overkill. They made a deadly team that was dangerously close. When cooperating, they acted like a single organism with more than double the destructive force of one Hippo on his own. If the Hippos weren't away on a mission, the assassin pair spent their days engaged in furious chess matches that almost always ended in stalemate. If either of them actually won a round, the other would accuse him of cheating and go sulk by himself for a while. The Doctor guessed the feelings were fleeting because the duo would end up in a heated rematch only minutes later. Despite being such efficient killing machines, the Hippos would never hurt each other.

The Doctor wondered how long their relationship would last.

Though the Twins shared the same exterior and a love of crushing spines, they were not exact doppelgangers. An Epitaph mandated brain scan of Hippo Number Two revealed that, even though his body's sculpting was complete, the nanobot sculptors still remained in the clone. Instead of a fully-functional, human brain, the robots built a specialized organ in the cranial cavity. This pseudo-brain had special receptors for the nanobots, allowing them to dock safely and communicate between one another, providing a form of temporary consciousness. They seemed to be tweaking Hippo Number Two's brain, programming their host with an incredibly diverse knowledge of worldly data and quirky personality traits. It wouldn't be long until Hippo Two became a walking encyclopedia, a braniac with two weapons of mass destruction on the tips of his arms.

Dr. Hadjaz worried that Hippo Number Two would even outstrip his own prized intellectual aspect. He wasn't progressing quickly enough on his assignment to suit his tastes, though the Epitaph himself hadn't made such exacting demands. His over-clocked brain began to fear for his career and personal safety. This super-clone could easily replace him given enough time! Hadjaz's worry quickly turned to fear and the fear evolved to panic. So, the Good Doctor did what any irrational being would do in his situation, he injected himself with serum and passed out in his sorely neglected bed.

filibuster

There were often times when President Ezra Gerrymander, leader of the Nation Formerly Known as the United States, wondered about his purpose. Not his grand, fire-in-the-sky kind of purpose, but the rote function of his job. In the recent era of peaceful Hegemony, his status had been reduced to that of an ambassador, a representative to attend the Summit of Nations. There were no wars left to fight and no edicts to be signed. The Hegemon and his cabinet dealt with all the important legislature and territorial sandwich disputes. The world had settled into an era of peace, for better or for worse.

The region governed by the President was currently known as the United State, singular. The people who lived there had grown fat and complacent, content to spend their lives watching videos of kittens biting young men in the face and baby turtles humping shoes. Ezra knew that, though it might seem peaceful, the world was growing dangerously stagnant. There was no fear, no urgency, and no drive toward excellence. The President felt like he had been given charge of a bloated carcass; a once great nation sat rotting in its own fluids, smelling slightly sweet like memories of marmalade.

The President was beginning to understand that his only real responsibility was to reflect an after-image of the great men gone before him, to instill tranquil pride in the hearts of his people. He would much rather be stirring their hearts, stoking the fires of Patriotism, with a capital P. In these languid days, Patriotism couldn't buy a taco off a fast food menu.

President Gerrymander had just finished eating dinner at his favorite restaurant in the whole District. At Rigotoni's, the food served was an Americanized bastardization of Italian cuisine. The President, without fail, ordered the shrimp linguini; he ate it weekly, every Sunday at six.

Ezra sighed. When had he fallen into such a droll routine? Picking excess exoskeleton from his teeth, the President mused that no soul was exempt from petrifying doldrums. He grinned, revealing his handiwork, perfectly clean incisors. Ezra Gerrymander was determined to make everything change before the night was over.

He made his way to his car, flanked by his two most trusted servicemen. Local gossip said that dangerous folks had been running wild through the District in recent days. The President didn't really follow that sort of drivel and he hadn't run into any loonies. Even so, he thought it was always nice to have an extra pair of guns on hand.

Suddenly, the world around the president slowed to a halt, like a slug crashing into a wall. His bodyguards froze midstep; they looked ready to fall over at any second. A family eating in the al fresco café nearby resembled a photograph, their faces petrified in masks of laughter. The President couldn't see what was so funny; he felt he was missing a joke. A tripping waitress was spilling chowder all over an obese customer's lap, but the meal levitated, hesitant to stain the pants of the man below it; the liquid dinner was paused like the rest of the world.

A figure appeared in front of the president, garbed in an oversized tweed robe. The hood of the robe obscured his face in shadow. From within that darkness came the light tenor of a young man.

"Are you the President of the United State?"

The President was terrified and excited, all at once. Had someone finally decided he was important enough to assassinate? The blood in his veins began to boil.

"Who are you? What do you want with me? What have you done to my men? What weaponry is this? I'm not going down without a fight, you terrorist!" He stepped forward and took a swing at the odd figure. The stranger easily dodged the President's wild blow with a quick step to the side. The motion revealed the man's feet; he was wearing sandals, simple and large. His feet were fleet, for someone wearing such clunky thongs.

"Mr. President, I'm sorry for the surprise. There was no other way to reach, erm, Your Highness. I just need to talk to you for just a few minutes."

"Don't try to sweet talk me, sugar." The President attacked again. He tried to distract the monk-like man with a feint to the right before striking from the left. This time, the monk didn't bother moving out of the way, he simply swatted the President's fist away like a drunken fly.

"Really, this would go a lot easier for both of us if you'd settle down. Please take this gesture as a sign of truce." The tweed-clad man reached up and pulled his hood away. Replacing the ominous darkness was a face full of sharp features, topped by a crop of short, blonde hair; it was greasy and unkempt. He appeared no more than fifteen years old, but spoke with the tongue of a much older man. "I'm so sorry for my appearance. Bob frowns upon those of us who haven't showered, but I've been awaiting your arrival for several days now. I'd hoped you would come a bit sooner."

The President stopped his assault, but kept his fists raised and his stance low, ready to launch a defensive maneuver. "Alright, let's talk. You're just a normal, everyday stalker, maybe. Everyone and their brother know I like Rigotoni's on Sundays. So you wanted to meet old President Gerrymander? Tell me what you're after, kid. And tell me what you did to these men!"

The mysterious man sighed with exasperation and tossed away his airs of mystery. "All right. I'm just borrowing some of their time. Don't worry, I'll give it back...eventually. Maybe. They probably won't even miss it if I don't. Look, I know it goes against your protocol, but it is imperative that I speak to you immediately."

The President squinted his eyes in concentration. This stranger was probably trying to confuse him. "What language are you speaking, boy? I don't know what protocol you're going on about. Are you an assassin?"

The hooded stranger let out a deep, irritated sigh. "No, I'm not an assassin. Surely, you realize I could have killed you ten hundred times already if that was what I wanted.

"My name is Jeremy. I am a Brother, Second Rank, in the Order of Builders. You haven't heard of us because you haven't needed to know about us until now."

This hurt the President's self-righteous feelings. "Well, who's to say that? I'm representative of nearly five percent of the world's population, damn it! If you're so important, I should be the first to know about... well... All right, what is it that you and your brothers do exactly?"

Ignoring the President's smarmy tone, Jeremy explained. His eyes lit up with the pride of a father showing off his daughter in her prom dress.

"Well, you could say that we're architects. You could also say that we're clockmakers. Maybe even artists. I guess you could say that we're a lot of things, but none of them would tell you exactly what we're doing. But see, what I do and who I work with and where I ate lunch...these things are not important. What is important is that we have an opportunity to save the lives of millions upon millions, depending on what happens tonight."

The President raised his eyebrows. "Millions of people? United State-ians?"

"Well, yes, actually. Among others. Not that it should matter." Jeremy took a deep breath and held it in for a moment, stopping himself from getting too flustered. "Here's the story. You were on your way to a secret meeting with a couple of representatives from other 'once glorious' nations, am I right? Some of your close friends from better times? Just a little get together before the Summit of Nations this weekend?"

"Yes, that is correct. How did you-"

"Mister President, if I let you get to that meeting, you're really going to screw the pooch. You're going to muck everything up for everyone you care about. And then some."

This was not what the President expected to hear. "Do you have something to back that up? It's a mighty powerful allegation you've got there.

Everything I do, I do for my country and her people."

"Mister President, just stop it. You're going to embarrass yourself. There are forces out there that you can't possibly imagine. Legions of chaos are playing a dangerous game with the fate of this world as the stake. A revolution is coming that will flip every truth you thought you knew upside down and round about. When chaos rules the land, your people will need someone to lead them, someone they can trust. Someone dead will do them no good.

"You are going to this clandestine meeting to vote on something very important with the other leaders, something that's been itching your legs for a long time. The ten of you are going to decide whether or not to secede from the Hegemony; I have orders to not let that happen under any circumstances. One nation after another will follow your example, until the Hegemony is shattered. War will blossom in such a garden, fertilized by blind pride and hurt feelings. I know this is exactly what you're looking for, but you are oblivious to the immediate repercussions. Lives will end, cut short by your selfish whim. Families will crumble; friends will cut friends by tooth and claw, all for the name of Mother Country.

"Then, things will get a whole lot worse. Chaos will flood the battlefield. Unstoppable, furious spirits will ride the winds as they seek out human blood. I can't even begin to describe how badly you should fear the reign of disorder.

"So, rather than try, I'm going to keep you here until your clique's secret vote is over and done. I can't risk you making the right decision on your own. Your presence at this meeting would have tipped the mood toward secession. Can you imagine? Just by being there, you would send the world into a spiraling nosedive of anarchy. Your aide is already present at the meeting and she will vote in your place once the other ambassadors are bored and tired of waiting. She will vote for peace, thank the Builder."

"How do you know all this?"

"You don't need to know the details. To put it simply, I took a loan on some loose time I saw floating about. I'd appreciate it if you kept that little tidbit to yourself. I didn't exactly follow the proper etiquette required of a lowly Brother like myself." Jeremy sighed, and shook exasperation out of his hair.

"Mister President, I've done what I needed to do. I've said all that I can really say. At least, I've said all that you'll understand. It's been three hours by my watch. Yours too, though that probably boggles your mind, doesn't it? Don't try to think about it too hard, your clock will sync up with the rest of the world before you can spell linguini. Those other ambassadors are an impatient lot, they've surely finished up the voting by now. I'll take my leave, if you don't mind."

The President didn't understand the first thing Brother Jeremy about what Jeremy meant by borrowing and lending time. He was perfectly fine with that.

Were his people really happy being lazy and carefree? Were they satisfied living their lives in mundane cycles, protected by general inaction throughout the world? He hadn't really put much value in that sort of lifestyle, but perhaps living a dull, peaceful life might be the best for everybody, after all.

"Wait! Jeremy, did I," he stammered, "Did we really just save millions of people?"

The monk smiled and turned to leave.

"May Bob provide you shelter wherever you may roam." With that simple blessing, Jeremy disappeared, fading away into the glowering dusk.

The world cranked back to life with a high-pitched pop, like a wishbone snapping. The president's bodyguards finished their half-steps and sprinted forward to catch up to their ward. A dining family continued chewing and swallowing and laughing. A waitress began profuse apologies before spilled soup could scald her panicked customer's lap. Everything was as it should have been all along, borrowed time slowly trickling back unnoticed into these innocent lives.

Abundantly, life flowed on, unfazed. Not a soul perceived that hours had disappeared, vanished in a heartbeat. Days later, after the time had finished returning to its previous owners, not a soul noticed the few minutes that were gone forever, stolen by a man in tweed.

Gyrations

Ophelia sat on the northern shore of Figment Isle, staring out into infinity. She stared as the setting sun sank below the horizon, a labyrinth of colors scattering through a partially cloudy sky. She liked to be near the roaring ocean waves; their static froth canceled out the constant buzzing in her head. The horizon was a blank slate, untainted oblivion. Ophelia rested her chin against her young chest and hugged her knees. Her gaze dropped lower and she lost herself in the tiny waves eagerly lapping at her toes.

The wavelets formed endlessly intricate patterns, dropping off and siphoning away grains of sand as they came and went. One wave rolled in gently, filling up a hole she dug between her feet. As the ebb flowed back to the sea, a miniature whirlpool was born in the puddle. Instead of returning to the ocean as one entity, the water scattered; it formed many tiny rivulets that got lost before they could reach the ocean, absorbed by the greedy sand beneath them. Ophelia frowned; she couldn't help but think of her family.

It felt good to get away from Castle Figment; the shining white fortress held too many opportunities for her to bump into her siblings. There was so much excitement bringing them close and so much ego driving them apart. This was supposed to be a time of celebration; the coming of Midas foreshadowed their escape from the island to rule the earth, sea, and stars. No galaxy would be unscathed, safe from the touch of the Creation Figment.

Still, her siblings fought amongst themselves, plotting ways to earn Midas' praise upon his return. Worse still, they talked about Ophelia behind her back. They called her unworthy, an unfitting conduit for their Master's gospel. It wasn't her decision to channel Midas; if she'd gotten her way, her brother Terra could have kept that blessing. It had only served to bring her grief. She was unsure if she even wanted Midas to return; he might have unreasonable expectations of her, his closest kin.

"It's been years since I've come to just sit and watch the ocean. It only takes an instant to remember why I loved it."

The warm, booming voice startled Ophelia, bringing her back to her self. "Oh, hello, Coelacanth. Yes, I like this spot. I come here often."

The strong, old man stood with his hands on his hips, gazing out at the setting sun. "I've spent a lot of time here, myself. I used to like to imagine myself as a sailor, free to travel the world and visit strange lands. Over the last few centuries, I've realized that my destiny awaited me here, not out there.

"I must admit, I miss the days when we could come and go as we pleased. I wish I didn't have to close the Threshold. Now our only connection to the outside world is that silly game our Father cooked up. We just cheer for the humans' self-destruction as we watch from the sidelines. Fat lot of fun that is, am I right?"

Ophelia shrugged. She'd never been a big fan of the game to begin with; now that her siblings couldn't stop talking about it, she actively disliked it.

"I suppose it's better that way," Coelacanth continued, "We shouldn't force ourselves into the lives of the humans. Their annihilation should be a product of their own wills, to make it more authentic. That's the way Midas wants it to be, and so it should be done. Even so, I miss walking the plains of Earth, watching the entropy accumulate firsthand. The smell of it crackling, the tingle is leaves on your tongue. You know what I mean?"

"I guess so. I don't know," Ophelia shrugged. She couldn't really relate to her brother's feelings. Being the most recent sacred vessel for Midas' word, Ophelia had never been allowed to leave Figment Island; she was much too precious. As a result, she had grown up knowing only her siblings, seeing only the grounds her feet could walk. A razor sharp reef surrounded the island, preventing her from leaving and visitors from arriving. She had never even seen a foreign ship out on the salty horizon.

"You know, when you came to us, we found you washed up on the shore. It was right over there." Coelacanth lifted his hefty, hairy arm and pointed at a spot less than twenty feet from where she sat. "All the others washed up on the south shore, but you were different."

Ophelia hugged her knees closer to her chest. "You don't have to remind me."

"I'm sorry," Coelacanth frowned. "What I meant to say is that you're special. You've got a gift, I can tell. When our Master arrives, and my heart tells me it will be soon, you will be the closest to him, the most blessed. Every one of us has, at one time, shared the connection to him that you currently posses. Every one of us has since lost it. There are those among your siblings who would kill to have it back."

"I just don't get it." Ophelia shrugged. "I don't understand any of this. Why am I the one who has to be special? Let Valkyrie be Master's radio, I didn't ask for this. I wish I could just fast-forward to the day Midas' returns and get him out of my head! I want to know who I really am, not whoever this voice inside me makes me think I am."

"Ophelia," Coelacanth sighed, his heaving breath condensing in the salty night air. "You are much too worried about the present. You must allow yourself to be excited for the future, proud of the past, and happy with the present all at once.

72

Nothing good will come from your worry. Everything will work itself out, eventually."

"Thanks," Ophelia said, "But I don't really know what to believe. I mean, I don't even know why we're trying to bring Midas back. What's the point?"

"Terra was partially right, you know," Coelacanth offered, "There are natural cycles of chaos and order. This universe began as pure order, all matter and reality condensed into a single point. The unavoidable flow of entropy has caused the universe to expand ever since that moment. With the arrival of our master and His great power, we will accelerate the growth of the universe to the point where everything is infinite. We will achieve a state of pure chaos. It will be a joyous day, when that finally happens.

"But the universe cannot remain like that forever. As soon as we reach that state, the flow of entropy will reverse. Everything will begin to condense, shrinking and regaining order until unity is achieved once more. Then the cycle will repeat itself. This reality we perceive is nothing more than a wave function of chaotic value. This is the way things have always been and probably the way things always will be."

Ophelia shook her head and began to trace and infinity in the sand. "That all sounds well and good. I mean, I love chaos as much as you, but what does it mean for us, as people? What happens after the waiting is over? And, why must we suffer so much as we wait for the day of reckoning? What's the point of all of this, Coelacanth? Can't you tell me that?"

Coelacanth sighed again, whispering through his bushy, white beard.

"I have lived for a very long time and I still can't answer that question. Time will tell us what we are meant to know. For now, just hold onto the faith that our Master will bring salvation to us all by purging the order from this place. Everything will end up as it is meant to be."

Ophelia wasn't satisfied, but talking with her oldest sibling always made her feel a little bit calmer. His voice was magical, and he was the only one who didn't resent her, even a little bit. "Thank you, brother. Will you stay to watch the tide go out with me?"

"I'm tired of the old man's philosophy lessons." Valkyrie leaned on a paw-paw tree in Castle Figment's orchard, eating a handful of paw-paw berries. In the orchard grew at least one hundred trees, bearing different fruit every season. "Everything will work itself out. Ha!" She snorted and spat a paw-paw seed on the ground. "I'm worried that little girl won't be ready to do her duty when the time comes. What do you have to say about that, fortune teller?"

Lazarus stood at the parapet, where he could see almost all of Figment Island. He had spotted the Coelacanth and Ophelia sitting on the beach and eavesdropped on their counsel. "Mmm, well, you know my visions haven't been all that clear these days. There's too much volatility in the balance of things. The good news is that probably means our Master will be here soon. Or it could mean we're all going to die. I really can't tell anymore."

"That's not good enough." Valkyrie spat again, just because she could. "I'm getting tired of waiting on the world to change. My destiny has got to involve more than just sitting around this castle. I've got so much damage to inflict but nowhere to do it." Her heavy boots ground freshly spit seeds into the loamy dirt.

Lazarus turned from the parapet. "You know, we could go over there. To the human realm. You have been to the human realm since the Threshold was closed, right?"

Valkyrie stomped the ground and pivoted to face her elder sibling, clenching her thighs like a rhinoceros about to charge. "What do you mean? Should I have been? The old man said we were trapped here!"

"Well, in a sense we are trapped here. But, of course, there is a way to get out there. Where do you think Archimedes gets the supplies for his endless stream of inventions? I go there myself once in a while, when I need to sow a little unrest or rattle some chains. Spread my seed, as it were. Come on, did you really think we were stuck here alone? How do you think I got myself such stylish duds?" Lazarus turned and shook his behind at his sister. He was wearing brown pants with red pinstripes to complement his ruby jacket. Despite his prophetic gifts, Lazarus was pathetically unable to predict next season's fashions.

"I don't like being lied to," Valkyrie said. A light in the Violence Figment's eyes shined, illuminating her fists in a hellish tint. "Why wasn't I informed of this? How do you get through?"

Lazarus gestured fervently that she should lower her voice. "Shhhh. Come on now, it's a secret. If the old fart knew I was telling you this, well, he'd be pretty ferocious. Only Archimedes, Coelacanth, and I know about the passage technique. The old man doesn't want us messing about where we don't need to. Supposedly, it's the word of Midas, right? Even so, I'm getting tired of just sitting around. I'm so bored and anxious."

"Wait a second," Valkyrie said, "I believe that old bastard knows how to get out of here, he knows too much that he's not sharing. I believe the science nerd figured out how to get off this island, too. What I don't understand, is why they would tell you. You're a moron among morons, brother."

"I'm not exactly sure how the transport works, but Archimedes tried to sell me something about time manipulation, blah, blah, blah. He always gets so caught up in his stupid jargon. Anyway, it turns out that my abilities are key. Since they needed to use my future sight, I forced them to tell me what my powers were being used for. They didn't realize that I could do it on my own once I learned how. I probably go out once a week or so. You don't even notice that I'm gone, do you, sis?"

Valkyrie pounded Lazarus hard on the back. "I don't like it, but I'm not going complain, brother. I need to push my limits and expand my boundaries. All right! Let's go, my fists are itching for some action!"

"All right, I'll take you just as soon as-"

A violent cough disrupted their exit. "You know, I can't really approve of you doing any of that."

Terra stood between the pair and the entrance to the castle. He was, as usual, completely bare, though he was accessorized by a hefty pair of hedge clippers.

"I was just coming up to do some yard work and what do you know, I find myself a couple of dirty hoes."

"Not a word of what we just said leaves this garden," Valkyrie's temper was quick to flare. "Do you hear me?"

"Whoa, whoa, whoa. Will you just wait and listen for a minute? Why do you feel some need to rush things, miss thundercloud? We'll get to the future when we get there and not a moment before. Don't you worry your pretty, giant head. Just give it some time.

"Now, seriously, when was the last time you stopped to smell the flowers out here? I've been doing some interesting crossbreeding and created one that smells like peanut butter nougat! Come here; check this out!"

"You know, your gardening habit has always bothered me," Valkyrie growled, ever militant. "You're growing advanced, highly organized organisms right here in our backyard. I call you a traitor! Doesn't it occur to you that you're fighting the pull of chaos when you tend to your plants?"

"No, man," Terra waved his sister's insinuations away. "You've got it all backwards. If I were doing this for any reason other than my own enjoyment, it would still be helping our cause. I mean, I'm running my own little chaos factory up here.

"Every living thing, you and these trees not excluded, is an entropy machine. When we eat and drink, we break down food to its simpler constituents. That alone is an unfathomable source of entropy, okay? Sure, some materials are recycled into ordered objects, but nothing is one hundred percent efficient. During each cycle, some energy and matter is lost to chaos and can never be recovered. In due course, nature will take us to a more entropic state.

"The humans of Earth have got it all down to a science. They consume and consume this planet's resources, turning it from a well-organized sphere to a burnt out husk. Frankly, they're quite lucky our Master is coming to liberate them soon. Otherwise they'd probably kill each other off, and then never experience the joy of pure chaos.

"With that said, I can't really support you going to change the natural order of things. It's not right. It's unnatural."

Lazarus stepped forward to stare his brother down. "Terra, I've got a good idea as to who among the humans is fighting the flow of chaos."

Terra smiled a mischievous grin. "Well, now. That changes everything. Why didn't you say something in the first place?" He gave his brother a hearty slap on the back and leaned his clippers against a tree. "I might not like it when you guys mess with nature, but I get downright furious when humans try to go against it. When do we leave?"

Lazarus glowered. His back was really smarting. "Let's depart immediately."

Round and round, Oedipus spun herself into a dizzy spell on a squeaky, padded stool deep in Castle Figment's dungeon.

"Would you stop that? I've already asked you about five hundred times. Ahem." Archimedes looked up from his workbench, covered in a messy array of wires and entropo-cubes. "If you knock over my equipment, well, I just might have to beat your bottom raw."

"Ooh, wee!" squealed Oedipus. "When can we start?"

"Look, I'm working on something that requires my full attention; I'm trying to figure out how the humans are buggering up our plans. Ahem. You know, something that will help our Master come back to join us?"

Oedipus allowed herself to slow to a stop before kicking herself into a spin in the opposite direction. "Gosh, I don't know. Starting up that game of ours seemed like such a foolproof plan. Use the humans as the unwitting tools of their own demise? Let the greedy little buggers eat away at their own civilization so we can come in and sweep away the remainder? Ah, brilliant. Our Master is a genius indeed."

"Yes, thank you. I get it. Ahem. Maybe we didn't enact the best of plans, yes, yes. What I mean to do is elucidate how the humans are stymieing us. Upon discovering that, ahem, we can do something to counteract it. Okay? Now please stop that spinning, thank-you-very-much!"

Not inclined to anything of the sort, Oedipus climbed on top of the spinning seat and took a standing position. She jumped and used momentum from her hips to accelerate the speed of her rotation.

"Oh, you do know how to keep a lady in suspense! Do tell me what you've got so far. What exactly have those nasty little mortals gotten away with?"

"Really? Ahem. You are quite the bother, aren't you? Alright. Squeaky joint gets the lube, as they say. Ahem.

"I," he began, "Don't know because you won't stop bothering me. Really, sister. You have got a knack for inspiring headaches of monstrous caliber. I'm going outside to clear my thoughts. I expect you gone when I return or I will sic some science on your ass."

Oedipus rolled her eyes. "Oooh, scary. Don't worry, I'm already gone."

Archimedes stormed away, leaving Oedipus alone in his lab. She waited several minutes as the shuffling sounds of feet trailed into the stuffy darkness.

"Thing is," she said, "You have no idea where I'm going."

She walked over to a doorframe in the corner of the lab. It was covered in a dusty blanket, apparently untouched for months. That layer of grime was a little trace of Oedipus' artistry, an illusion to distract her family from the discovery that she alone was meant to know. This doorframe was Oedipus' secret portal to the land of mortals; as far as she knew, it worked only for her.

Oedipus had gone through many times before, always returning within a day or two. This time, she didn't know when she would be back. Her heart began to pound harder hard as she lifted her foot. It felt as heavy as iron, fighting her every stride. There was too much risk in this foolhardy endeavor, she could lose everything and hurt her family, too. But, she realized, that was the point, after all.

A burst of confidence broke the spell on her feet, and she pressed forward. The battles ahead would be difficult, but everything started with a single step. She leaped through the threshold and the world began to spin.

The Epitaph was returning to her kingdom.

Hyperbolic

A would-be assassin lay sprawled on the bed, steam rising out of the three bullet wounds on his chest. Petyr stood in the bathroom doorway, still sopping wet from his shower. The barrel of his gun radiated a powerful heat, burning his palms like one thousand dying suns. It had been nearly three months since he'd quit the game and gone rogue, an eternity in the life of a secret agent. It was about time the Minotaur sent another hitman after him. This attempt had been much too easy to foil; could his old employer really take him so lightly?

His escape from the dungeons of Dom Com had been relatively easy. She had kept him chained up and tortured him regularly for about a week, but her spirit wasn't in it. With no secrets to pry out of him, the whole scenario was ruined for her. Revenge was only sweet if there was something there to taste. After ten days, she let him go free. She promised that it wouldn't be their final encounter, but Petyr direly hoped she was wrong.

For the next few weeks, he had spent his time flitting from city to city, all across Europe. He knew of a number of hiding spots with friendly contacts that he had made through during his tenure as a secret agent. These places he avoided at all costs, certain that traps would wait near his known affiliates.

Petyr traveled by train, as hitchhiker, and even on horse to the dark corners of the world, taking care never to stay in one place for more than a few days. The entire essence of Petyr Dmitriev was devoted to staying out of trouble and under the radar of his enemies. Occasionally, a pursuer would catch him but they were always quickly dispatched.

Petyr felt he had wasted a lot of time and effort if this was the best assassin his foes were going to send at him. So much time, gone forever; he could never get it back.

Without bothering to hide the deceased mercenary, Petyr dressed himself and repacked his sole backpack. It was time to move again.

Petyr was currently hiding in Prague, a city he hadn't visited for several years. As a child he had longed to visit here, but was only able to read about it in books. The mystery and majesty of the cities history combined to transport his malleable young mind to a world of fantasy. The golems and faeries and ghosts of Czech lore had all fascinated him for years, until he finally visited the city on an undercover assignment. Seeing the sights and hearing the stories from local perspectives, he ultimately understood that the myths were only make-believe. His dangerous lifestyle required that he harden his heart and hone his mind so as to separate fantasy from reality. These days, his decisions were based in cold hard logic, usually.

He wasn't sure why he had come to Prague, a high-traffic city surrounded by a sea of unfamiliar territories. He could have easily gone north to the Hinterlands or south to the Saharan deserts. Both would have hidden him more completely. Something had drawn him back here, to this city from his memories.

Petyr enjoyed the intricate architecture, the simple but hearty food, and the complex maze of streets winding through the castle district. It was all exactly as he remembered. Prague was not a city to change quickly; it remained much the same as it was centuries before. Petyr even appreciated the grandeur of the Saint Vitus Cathedral, despite his aversion to God in all His trappings. He walked the holy grounds, trying to count the different gargoyles in their perches on high. Petyr was so rapt in thought that he didn't feel the first knife until it was scraping against his tibia.

He dodged the second by a fraction of a hair, feeling its sharp blade cut through the air by his ear. How foolish he had been! It was a textbook play; send in the true professionals after the amateur is sacrificed. Petyr, the target, had let his guard down. He deserved the injury, but he didn't plan on dying here.

He turned and rolled to safety, quickly righting himself to a battle stance. He immediately fell to his knees, his hamstring utterly useless. He clenched his teeth and prepared for the next cut. It never came.

Petyr opened his eyes to see the pair of thugs attacking him frozen midswipe. A man, garbed in grey, stood on the tips of his toes, like he was about to spring into a desperate leap. A girl with a bloody knife balanced on one foot, lunging forward with her whole body weight. Their poses were impossible, gravity should have taken its toll, but they remained erect. Petyr looked around, there was not another soul in the courtyard, but he saw birds above him paused in flight.

"Hey, Petyr! Hey! Come here!"

A strange man dressed in tweed robes was urgently beckoning to Petyr from an alcove behind him.

"Hey! Hey! Come with me, Petyr Dmitriev! If you want to see another sunrise, that is. I mean, well, if you want there to be another sunrise. I mean, oh, just come on already."

Something felt very wrong, but Petyr's mind was racing too fast to question the situation. He hobbled over to the short man; that leg was going to cripple him for a while.

"I'm very sorry about that," the strange man took Petyr's arm and gave him some stabilizing support. "I knew your name, but I didn't know your face. It was unfortunate, but necessary, that those thugs attack you. I knew I was going to meet you today, but I wouldn't have been able to tell your face from a Rottweiler's hiney. All I knew was that I had to save Petyr Dmitriev, who would be attacked in this courtyard. So, uh, I guess I could've saved you from that knife, but, well, whoops!

"Pardon me. I never introduced myself. My name's Jeremy. I'm a member of the Order of Builders. Here, let me fix that, it's bothering me." The man grabbed Petyr's knee before he could do anything to protest. Jeremy appeared to be focusing intently, staring at the wound and wishing it away.

"Hey, what are you doing?" Petyr started. He was cut off by a terse shush.

"I'm healing you. Be quiet for a second."

Petyr's leg felt strange and tingly. When the monk stood, Petyr saw that his wound had vanished completely.

"What? Where did it go? What exactly did you do to me?"

The monk smiled. "I just took away some of that time your leg just experienced, replaced it with some better time. See! It's all better!"

Petyr felt like this man was speaking an entirely different language, but he had certainly worked a miracle. Wounds didn't just disappear on their own. "Okay, let me rethink my previous question. What are you, exactly?

"I wish I could explain easily," Jeremy started. "I've been getting that question a lot, lately. Until now, nobody has really needed to know the answer, but you're important. I'll give it my best shot. Let's walk while we talk."

The duo ducked into a dark, decrepit doorway at the back of Jeremy's alley. When they passed through the threshold, Petyr stopped. He suddenly found himself staring at the rock walls of a long dark tunnel. Sporadically, torches lit the path.

"How did we-?" Petyr started.

The monk cut him short. "I showed you what I can do with time; you think that I can't do it with space too? I'm not entirely a creature of your world, Petyr. It is utterly important that you understand that, right now, okay? I am a projection of a much more complicated beast. Well, you see me as a monk, an ascetic, or whatever you want to call it, but those words do not describe who or what I am. Certainly, this body you see before you is human. I am full of brains and guts and emotions, just like you. In flesh and form, we are no more different than two breeds of dog.

"Come on." Jeremy started walking down the tunnel, leisurely. Petyr looked over his shoulder to see only tunnel. The doorway had morphed into nothingness. He had no choice but to follow his strange companion.

"What separates us is that I perceive this world in a fundamentally different way than you do," Jeremy said. "This body is but a tiny tendril extending from a much greater whole. I am merely the fingertips of a bigger body. A much bigger body. That greater whole extends through multiple dimensions, but your perception of this universe only supports a few of them, so you see me as a simple ascetic.

"To the source of my consciousness, whom I call Bob for convenience, time is a trivial thing. He perceives what you and I call time the way our eyes might see a blob of Play-Doh. He can observe all the time that has existed or will ever exist, all at once. His visions trickle down to me through my dreams, his will is manifested through my actions.

"With that in mind, do you see where my powers come from? I can rearrange any bits of existing time because time is nothing but a toy, a big puzzle that can be put together an infinite number of ways. If ever I need to pause, fast-forward, rewind, or otherwise manipulate time, Bob can allow me to do that. But really, my abilities are merely fleas compared to the elephants of Bob's powers. My three dimensional brain can't begin to truly comprehend his greatness. Yours either, so don't waste your time."

"I don't get it. You're telling me you're some sort of demigod? A disciple of a multidimensional entity?" Petyr asked, wary of the math that might be involved in further conversation. Things were getting weirder and weirder, but Petyr knew he should just ride this wave until it took him back to a world of sanity. He was certain he wouldn't find it in this tunnel.

"Well, yeah, okay. That's an all right word for it, though I don't like the implication that I'm not human. I am most certainly a human being. I'm just a little bit, you know, different. My earthly vessel, like your own, has an expiration date. Everybody and everything has to die sometime, right?

"Thing is, normally, humans travel through time forward in a series of straight lines; their vectors of perception pass through all the events they are destined to experience, all neatly arranged into this globular mass of time. They continue on their journey, occasionally crossing paths with and joining up with other temporal travelers, until they finally die.

"I am detached from that artifice, my version of time goes both ways. I can remember my whole existence, from cradle to grave. My memories go right up until the moment of my death; I don't usually think about that horribleness except for when it's actually happening. I've never actually experienced death, mind you. It's like my life is a hyperbola, I will never know the truth beyond that last bit of my time. Everyone in my order is like that."

"Wait a second. There are more people like you?"

The monk smiled his well-practiced grin of enlightenment. "Yes, of course. We are the Order of Builders. All of us are builders of some kind; we live to create complexity out of simplicity, order out of chaos. We fight the flow of entropy. There are chemists and cooks and writers and architects among us. I personally get no greater satisfaction than building the perfect footstool.

"But those are just our day jobs." His voice took on a heroic timbre. "We oppose the generation of chaos in this world. I like to think of us as the Guardians of Eternity." His pomp quickly deflated. "But, well, something big and bad is happening. There's a bit of time that's tainted with something bad, it's untouchable. We can't move it; we can't get our minds around it.

"If the rest of time were a big lake, reflecting all that has occurred or will occur, this bit of time is a brick that has crashed through the water's surface. It's sending distorted ripples throughout the rest of eternity. We can't see exactly how big it is or know how long it will last. It's a tumor among an otherwise perfectly healthy system, growing and spreading out of my vision and reach. I want to purge it from the body of time, but I don't know how.

"No matter what I try to do, I can't touch it, move it, or even see around it. It's like someone put blinders on me and I can't see where I'm going. Even Bob isn't sure exactly what to do. Or, if he does, he hasn't told any of us. Honestly, I've never been so frightened. "

"I don't understand. What does that mean?" Petyr wasn't following Jeremy's logic. Metaphysics wasn't covered with much emphasis during agent basic training.

"Have you ever had a nightmare? Have you even woken up to a cold sweat, to escape the monsters of your dreams? Petyr, those monsters are going to come here and they are more horrible than you can possibly imagine. They are going to devour everything: space, time, and Bob himself! They will make it as though we've never existed."

"Sure, I've had nightmares before. I used to have them all the time as a kid. You expect me to believe my childhood nightmares are suddenly going to become real? They're going to come and eat up time? What? Are you kidding me? Come on. I'll grant you, something weird is going on. You did something crazy to my leg, you did something to those assassins and the birds, but the thought nightmares becoming real is just silly."

"It's true! You've got to believe me. This fluctuation of time indicates that the father of chaos is coming here! He's going to destroy our world in a manner most terrible. It will not be a quick and painless death for any of us. Those nightmares in your childhood were simply his envoys, messages from the dark beyond. He was seeking out our greatest fears so he can employ them against us.

And that's the least of our troubles. I can't even begin to explain the chaos our world will experience on its way to the end. It's beyond comprehension! Every fundamental tenet of reality will cease to exist as we understand it."

Neither of the pair said anything; they walked in silence for several minutes. Petyr would have run away if he had any idea where he was located. He had entered an awkward zone where he was utterly uncomfortable. Suddenly, the monk broke the silence.

"I have a terrible confession to make, on behalf of my brothers and myself. Our methods of fighting the chaos haven't exactly been very pure. We have been siphoning time from people around the globe. A few minutes here, a few minutes there. Not enough that anyone would actually notice. Five minutes times five billion people equals an eon or two. I know it sounds terrible, but we used the time to pad a layer around the growing darkness, attempting to construct a barrier that would delay the coming of chaos until we could find a way to fight it."

"So?" Petyr asked. "Who cares if they lose a few minutes of time? It's better than losing everything for eternity, or whatever you think is supposed to happen."

"Well, that's what we were thinking," Jeremy said, "But really, we've been eroding our victims wills, you know? That's sort of a cardinal sin, in our book. By spending their time on our own agenda, we robbed people of their right to choose how they would spend those minutes. Free will is the holiest of holy blessings, and it's not right to deny that to any person."

"So, how did you heal my leg?" Petyr was beginning to make some sense of this situation, or at least the words coming out of Jeremy's mouth. "Did you steal those minutes from me for this grand cause?"

Jeremy nodded excitedly. "Well, yes! You've almost got it. I actually gave your leg a bit of time from someone else's leg."

"So, there's someone else out there whose hamstring suddenly split in two? That sucks. I mean, I appreciate your help certainly, but you're kind of a jerk."

Jeremy scowled. "I can give you your own time back, if you'd rather have it."

Petyr shrugged. "No, no. It's all right. I'm okay."

"That's what I thought," Jeremy said smugly. "Well, I took the time from a soldier who was dying anyway. He'll hardly notice." He shrugged, as if this explanation made his actions seem alright. His smile turned slightly bittersweet. "I thought that if we were able to find a way to fight the chaos, as long as we could stave it off, we could justify our choices to Bob. Unfortunately, despite everything we've done, the world has reached a tipping point. The agents of chaos could arrive any day now.

"Petyr, you must help me, for the sake of the universe's continued existence. A thousand galaxies might birth and fade before a man of your abilities will walk this earth again."

"I have no idea what abilities you could possibly think I have." The normally unshakable Petyr Dmitiriev was feeling a little anxious about the situation. He wasn't sure if the man he was speaking to was absolutely crazy or unimaginably sane. Jeremy definitely had powers that Petyr didn't understand, and it worried him. "Look, I still don't know if I believe you about all this 'struggle against chaos' and nightmare stuff, but I'll admit that you've got some strange abilities. Me? I've got nothing. I'm just a washed up spy who's on the lam. One false move and my enemies will slit my throat or shoot me in the back. Your enemies? Well, it seems like they're supposed to destroy reality itself. What could I possibly do to help in this situation?"

"I don't know." The monk stopped and frowned at Petyr. "Really, I'm very sorry. Like I said, I didn't even know your face when I was supposed to meet you. My temporal vision has blurred so much I don't even know what I'm going to eat for dinner! I'm sure it won't be long before we have to find out these answers the hard way. Well, I guess it's the normal way for you. For now, I think you should meet my brothers and we should get some food in our bellies. It will make things easier for us, in the long run. I think. Ah, here we are."

They had arrived at a great wooden door, inlaid with ornate metal sculptures of clocks. One clock at the center of the door looked like it had working parts, but it had stopped moving. Something about the door inspired an ominous feeling of evil; both Petyr and Jeremy could feel it and glanced at each other.

"I don't understand," Jeremy began. "It's supper time. My brothers should be enjoying Father Randolph's cooking and making merry. I don't smell or hear anything."

Petyr's agent instincts kicked in fast; he pushed Jeremy aside, shushed the monk, and sidled up to the door. He had pulled his gun without realizing a need for it. As quiet as ever, he slowly pulled the door open and peered in cautiously.

The Brotherhood was at dinner, but the entree had been served as a cold dish. Sitting at a long wooden table were the bodies of thirty men, all dressed in the garb of the Order of Builders. Most of the monks were slumped forward onto the table, but a few had fallen over backwards onto the floor.

Petyr didn't have to check the bodies to know that all the Brothers were dead.

Jeremy was getting nervous. "What's in there? What's going on?"

Petyr pulled himself away. "I'm sorry, I don't know how to say this, but-"

It was too late for words. The overeager monk darted around his companion to enter the room. As soon as he passed the threshold, he tripped and fell to his knees before slumping onto the floor. He clawed at his skull like a hundred angry spirits were tickling his brain but he couldn't get in to scratch it. The monk writhed on the ground for several moments, before unleashing an unearthly scream.

"Oh, it's here; the ominous moment is imminent! All our work has been for naught."

He rolled onto his backside, turning to look at Petyr while madness gleamed in his eyes.

"The Reign of Chaos has come at last! Petyr, the stars ordained our meeting. Now is the time for your destiny to come to pass. You must accept your fate and fight the coming darkness. Will you accept your destiny?"

Petyr wanted to answer this man's call for help, but couldn't muster the stamina. This was far beyond his tolerance for weirdness. "I have no idea what you're talking about."

Ingrate

The Hippo loved his new situation. His job was fun, the pay was fair, and Epitaph Industries provided free all-you-can buffets every Friday. He couldn't have hoped for a better gig.

On top of all that, he'd gotten something incredible, something he had never expected to want. The part of his job that The Hippo loved best about his was his new best friend and brother, The Hippo. The Hippo always seemed to know exactly what The Hippo was thinking; they never had to fight about anything.

Nothing made him happier than getting to play a game of chess with his brother. They were on a quest to play the perfect game. Many people didn't consider the game an art form, but the Hippo knew better than them. A pair of dancing wills locked in an epic battle of wits was the epitome of beauty.

The Hippo loved his work as well as his leisure. He savored every bone-crunching minute of his missions. When two skulls banged together, they resonated with such a pretty tone, riddled with harmonics that most people never experienced. It was even better now that he had someone who appreciated it just as much as he did, someone with whom he could share the secret joys of destruction.

The Hippo looked up from the chessboard to smile at his brother; the Hippo smiled back. Though he wasn't much for superstition, The Hippo knew he had found his soulmate.

He was especially grateful that his associate, the Doctor, had been keeping to his own devices of late. That man was far too busy of a body, always rushing off to complete his next assignment, to meet his next deadline. He was constantly thinking of his next goal and the goal after that, never stopping to enjoy the work he was doing while he was doing it.

The Hippo's rare interactions with the Doctor had gotten exceptionally irritating since the scientist had taken the bifurcation serum. After he successfully made himself one brother, he made a dozen more. That left him with way too many brothers for the Hippo to bother counting.

After his first brother was born, the Doctor had asked the Hippo a lot of annoying questions. The Hippo didn't pay him much attention, because everything the Doctor said reminded the Hippo of a hungry gnat. Their conversations always went along the lines of: "Why didn't you tell me this? Why didn't you tell me that? I'm overly excitable!"

The Hippo's answer was always very simple. "The Hippo never told ya, 'cause the Doctor never asked."

The Hippo bobbed his massive head, shaking the unpleasant thoughts out of his austere brain. The Doctor wasn't worth the worry he inspired. Too much anxiety was going to ruin this chess match. This game was the closest he and his brother had come to achieving a perfect game, a master-class round of strategic warfare. Every round brought them a little bit closer to the consummate game.

The Hippo took a deep breath to bring his focus back to the chessboard. The Doctor caused the Hippo only frustration. Frustration destroyed inner peace. Without inner peace, life was not worth living. Chess made life worth living. When the Hippo exhaled, all his bad thoughts went out with the stale air.

This morning, the Doctor was especially excited and anxious. He was packing up various instruments and devices as quickly as possible. His brothers moved efficiently, stacking and ordering boxes of varying size and weight.

There was most certainly an unapproved operation underway. The Doctor had begged the Hippo to keep quiet about it. He said that if the Epitaph found out, he would certainly be angered. The Doctor had nothing to worry about from The Hippo.

When the Doctor declared he was taking his brothers away to start a bigger lab, The Hippo couldn't have been happier. Finally, he would have a tranquil place to spend his days with his own brother. Normally, The Hippo was all in favor of blind loyalty to a fat wallet, but he was willing make an exception in this case. He hoped it didn't make a difference in the long run.

A knock at the door caused all the bustling Doctors to halt in their tracks. The clone closest to the door cautiously, silently opened it.

Four masked soldiers holding semi-automatic machine guns hustled through the portal, forming a line of offense in the lab. Their torsos were protected by black, Kevlar body armor; the rest of their bodies were completely covered by pieces of dark, chitinous ceramic. Their dark helmets completed an insect illusion, reflecting images of the many Doctors like a compound eye. These men were obviously professional and deadly serious. The Hippo reckoned he or his brother would probably get shot a few times before he could take them all out. That seemed like a rather unpleasant situation.

A young woman came forward from behind the soldiers. Her zebra striped dress fit like paper-mache, clinging to her body's every curve. The eyes she laid upon Dr. Hadjaz glinted with a sparkle of mischief. Every clone gulped down a mouthful of nervous bile; something about the woman's attitude made the Hippo feel his future had gotten significantly less bright.

"Hey there, Doc. It's nice to meet you in person, finally. I'm the Epitaph, by the way. A pleasure, I'm sure." She walked up and down the line of soldiers, pacing furiously.

"Doc, you're a good scientist. The best. I hired you because I know that and you know that. But I've gotten to worrying that you're maybe a little bit too good. Out of control, maybe? Too good for your own good, that's for certain. I'm concerned that you've been keeping secrets from me, doing research that you might not want me to know about. Maybe you're not following my orders? Is there anything you want to tell me?"

The Doctors mumbled a few aimless syllables. Their plans were dissolving faster than a hamster in a microwave.

The Epitaph turned from the closest Doctor clone to another hiding behind a stack of boxes. "What about you, you know anything? How about you? Oh my, you all look mighty similar.

"This is pretty upsetting, Doc. You're using my resources, my fat wallet, but you're keeping me in the dark. Come on, you know how I'm afraid of the dark. Actually, I guess you don't, and I'm not, but that's neither here nor there. Oh, I'm getting beside myself. I hope you can see how this is a little bit embarrassing for me."

The Doctor finally managed to obtain some form of composure. "Ah, yes. Of course. I mean, I didn't mean. I was going to do a report on all of this, I swear it. I just needed a little more time to figure things out. I just need a few more data points, I swear."

The Epitaph cut him off. "I don't know exactly what you've been up to, but it looks like something's been rather successful. I like to reward successes, so I'm going to overlook your recent behaviors, m'kay? In exchange, I need you to help me out with one little experiment I've been dying to explore."

She put her hands on her voluptuous hips and beamed a sultry smile. "So, which one of you is the original Doctor?"

The Good Doctor and his clones stood speechless; overwhelming fear had suddenly incited an epidemic of dry mouth. This woman was more volatile than a cask full of gunpowder perched precariously over a line of flamethrowers; the unstable barrel was a lot less likely to explode.

"Not a word. That's too bad." The Epitaph reached deep between her cleavage and pulled out a large, black pistol. Without a moment's hesitation, she leveled her arm and shot the closest Doctor between the eyes.

He died instantly; the shock from his death traveling through the psychic link back to the Good Doctor and out into all his remaining twins. Dr. Hadjaz doubled over and started pushing on his temples, trying to squeeze out the pain. All eleven remaining clones clutched at their foreheads and emitted pain-stricken moans. The Epitaph had dispensed a migraine to end all migraines.

She stood and watched them writhe in pain. "Still going to stay silent? Nobody will come forward as the real Good Doctor? Well, there's plenty more where that came from." The Epitaph extended her arm and unloaded twice, one bullet each between the eyes of a pair clones.

"Doctor, Doctor, give me the news. I've got a bad case of shooting you!" The delirious crime lord was bobbing her head and dancing as she sang, eyes shut tight.

Bang, bang, bang, click, click. Three more clones fell to the ground as she discharged the last of her bullets.

"Aww. There are a lot more of you than I realized. It's a good thing I planned ahead." The Epitaph grabbed a gun from one of her guards and took aim. A faint click resounded as she released the safety.

Time seemed to slow, unfolding itself one hundred times, then one hundred times again, as the Epitaph loaded bullets into the Doctor's treasured twins. One by one, he watched as his brothers fell to their knees; he saw his own brains spatter on the ground. Copies of his face twitched in agony, their last gasps spewing psychic waves to pierce his heart and drain him of his empathy. The voices of his dying companions slowly accumulated in his consciousness, their collective cries driving him closer to the precipice of madness. Suddenly, he was alone among strangers. It looked as though a mirror had been broken and shattered on the floor, reflecting his ultimate destiny.

But he was not alone. The spirits of his fallen blood whispered sweetness directly into his brain, begging him to come join them in the astral plane. Though unpierced by bullets, the Good Doctor was a shattered man.

The Epitaph strutted over to the Doctor as he knelt on the ground, hands pulling at his hair. His face was a reflection of the death masks around him, straying from perfection by his twitching lips and tear-stained cheeks.

"Hey Doc, it looks like I'm not done with you, yet. No, sir. It wasn't a coincidence that I left the real you alive. I've been watching closely, bub. You and I are entwined by fate, and I could tell from your pain that you were the genuine article.

"I've got at least one more bullet stowed away, but it's not for you, not yet. You may have tried to screw me over, but I've still got one last project for you. This is going to win the game for real! I'm not even talking about Anonymous anymore. I'm aiming much, much bigger. If you can pull this off, well, maybe I'll even forgive you. Probably not, but maybe! Isn't that great?"

The Doctor replied with a mumbled groan, a wordless cry for mercy. "Aww, that's so cute. You're totally useless right now. It's a good thing I have someone else to talk to or I'd be going mental." The Epitaph removed herself from the pitiful scientist.

"Hello, Misters Hippo. I haven't forgotten about you. I have-oh my." The Epitaph stopped in her tracks, ceasing her approach. Her face turned pallid, the blood drained completely. Her expression contorted itself into a bizarre conglomeration of fear, hilarity, and agony. She paused a moment to recover her composure. "Misters Hippo, err, Dancing Hippos, you have been nothing but loyal during your tenure with me. I want to reward you with an extra special mission. Before I tell you what it is, I need you to promise you will obey, no matter what. Can you do that for me?"

The Hippo looked up from chessboard, acknowledging his boss. The gunfire and slaughter had been a faint distraction, white noise behind the curtain of his concentration. Even so, something about the atmosphere was ruined; the wailing of The Good Doctor was certainly annoying. His mood was ruined. This chess match couldn't possibly be the perfect game for which he was questing.

"The Hippo is here only to serve," he said.

The Epitaph smiled, as color slowly returned to her features. "Good. That's very good news. I'm so grateful." She heaved with relief; the fear that had gripped her tightly a few minutes ago seemed to have dissipated completely with The Hippo's response.

"Mister Hippo, I need you to follow these instructions to the letter." She passed him a slip of paper, neatly folded and sealed with wax. "Are there going to be any problems carrying out your duty?"

The Hippo opened the order and quickly glanced through its contents. He discovered a very powerful reason to smile and he unleashed his massive gums upon the room. He and his brother laughed together, emitting big booming guffaws that shook the world around them. Their chess match was utterly ruined, all the pieces scattered by their joyous vibrations. At the bottom of the commands, below a lengthy list of most complicated directions, one phrase stood out. These were words that the Hippo had longed to hear: Kill the Good Doctor.

"No ma'am. No problems for the Hippo."

"Good. Remember, these instructions must be followed, down to the very last punctuation mark. I need you to get started immediately. It may already be too late for you to do any good."

The Hippo ignored this last comment. His mind was already spinning with the many possible ways the Doctor might fall by his hands. "With pleasure."

Oedipus stepped outside, desperate for a breath of fresh air. The Doctor's lab smelled like his terrible body odor; the fresh scent of murder made it smell only a little better. Masquerading as the Epitaph was growing more stressful every day, but it was her only chance of achieving her goals. If she could continue the charade a bit longer, she would become Hegemon and have access to all the world's power. She would finally have everything she needed.

Oedipus dismissed her guards, ordering them to escort the gibbering Doctor back to her headquarters. His temporary safety was important if the rest of her plan was to continue without any hiccoughs. There had been one too many surprises already. Her heart was still beating fast from the mental ravaging she had experienced inside the laboratory. Midas was coming, sooner than she had anticipated. His proximity sent psychic ripples to all his kin; that ripple had nearly torn Oedipus apart. It was a terrifying thought; her Master was finally going to arrive. By taking part in the game her Lord had devised, she was defying his direct order to avoid interfering with the human realm. Chances were good that Oedipus was going get a very nasty punishment when her Father got home.

Jaundice

A few seconds passed before Petyr and Jeremy realized they were not alone. An urgent din arose in the kitchen adjoining the dining hall. Petyr put his fingers to his lips and pressed his ear to the door.

A few muffled curses coupled with more crashing and clanging escaped through the wooden barrier. With a deep breath, the well-trained agent followed his instincts, kicking open the door, his weapon at the ready.

"Oh, oh, my! Don't shoot, don't shoot." An old man dressed in the Order of Builders' tweed robes was balancing precariously over a messy pile of grimy pots and pans.

At the sound of that voice, Jeremy rushed past Petyr into the room. "Father Timothy! Oh, thanks be to Bob." The young man embraced the old monk, gripping his torso like a bear trap. "I'm so glad to see you."

Petyr felt something strange take root inside the pit of his stomach; a foreign signal climbed up his spine. *Aliens infest my blood, my space, are taken to my leader.* He blinked the odd feeling away.

"And I am glad to see you, my son. Thank the Builder you were away on assignment during this catastrophe." The older man's voice had a soft edge, a warm blanket of sound to temper the hottest nerves. Jeremy began to relax, tension slipping away as the baritone elixir allayed his anxieties.

Jeremy lowered his head and frowned. "I suppose I am lucky. It doesn't seem as though I could have done anything at all. All of our brothers killed at once? A mighty foe has risen. The rise of chaos touches us all." Jeremy glanced up at his mentor. A shimmering sparkle marked the young man's eyes. "We have spent our lives getting ready for this day, and I still do not know how I am supposed to act. I want to stop, to mourn my family, but I know there is too much to do. If I allow myself to weep now, I might never recover. We were ingrained to fight the legions of chaos until our last breaths escape. We must struggle on for the sake of the Order. For Bob! For all order!

"Father, you survived this massacre. Please, share with us how you escaped the slaughter of our kinsmen? Let us take this strategy to Midas himself."

Timothy sighed and shook his elder head. "My son, I am ashamed to tell you this, but I was hidden away during the whole attack, trapped by my own cowardice. I ask your forgiveness, because it is not quite as simple as that. Please allow me to explain my actions, for fear you think me a spineless thug.

"Most of the Order was settling in for one of Brother Bristol's songs. I was assisting in Randolph's dinner preparation by cleaning the necessary dishes and cookware. The Brothers were just finally quieting down when the door to the dining hall was busted through. Three wretched creatures appeared, exploding into the room with roars and spit.

"Their obvious leader was a tall gentleman, dressed in a dandy's outfit. He was accompanied by a testosterone-fueled amazon and a lackadaisical, naked man. Though they formed an unlikely team, the trio exuded tremendous power; it was obvious that they had come with the intention to punish us for some reason. I had a sinking feeling they would let none of us escape alive.

"So, I panicked and quickly concealed myself behind a thin veil of time. Oh, I tried to help our brothers but I couldn't touch a bit of the temporal substance in the dining room. I could sense that one of the invaders had some power to counteract my own, a gift on the level of Bob's might! I was helpless! Impotent! I was reduced to being an observer, unable to assist, forced to watch as my dearest ones were butchered.

"The nudist began a dance that somehow hypnotized our Brothers; they were glued to their seats, staring blankly as these devils commenced to kill them. The warrior woman pummeled each one of our brothers until their skin began to split. Nobody reacted at all! None of our kin were able to fight. Nobody even screamed in fright. They were completely enthralled by the nudist's dance. Meanwhile, the dandy fop just smirked and watched his cronies commit heinous acts. He must have been the one with the power to cancel my abilities, I'm sure of it. That air he carried, that pompous aura. It was as though he knew there was no threat to his minions.

"Oh Jeremy. None of them had a chance to escape. Once he was satisfied that we were all dead, the tall devil ordered his cronies to stop their mutilation. They searched the kitchen for survivors but I was already hidden behind my veil. I tried to stop them, to freeze them, to hurt them, but I couldn't do a thing. I couldn't even reveal myself. Apparently, the fop's power only prevents time manipulation in its presence; it doesn't cancel out any manipulation that has already occurred. Otherwise, I'd be as dead as the rest of them. If I ever run into him again, I-"

The charmed reunion was interrupted by a loud clatter. Petyr had dropped his pistol into the cluster of kitchenware. His hands were shaking violently and his eyes were bulging out of his skull. As the two monks stood by, Petyr collapsed, falling forward into the pile of pots and pans.

A burning flame sprouted from Petyr's gut, rising up his throat to the back of his mouth. *One hundred thousand shadows converge, blocking all the light and feasting on my memories.* As Petyr vomited and his vision faded, he glimpsed a huge, black moose lunging at his face, gnashing jaws ready to tear his heart to shreds.

The two monks carried Petyr to an unused bed. His temperature had risen far beyond the dangerous level; his body was a furnace about to melt itself away. Beads of sweat collected on his brow, as wrinkled as an angry elephant. The pallor of his skin was a sick yellow, like a freshly painted egg. Jeremy tried to cover his acquaintance with a sheepskin blanket, but the fevered agent wouldn't stay still.

"Quit your wiggling, you stupid ass. I'm trying to do you a favor." The young Brother was frustrated, his words laced with flakes of spittle.

"Jeremy! Such language. Please remember, you are in our sacred home now, not on the streets of the unwashed masses. Please, Brother, you must calm yourself. This is the man who is supposed to protect us from the Lord of Chaos. Don't be angry with our savior." Father Timothy's soothing voice reached out to pet his disciple's agitated soul.

Jeremy would have nothing of the sort, slicing through the baritone with squeaky rage. "This man? This secret agent? He's nothing but a weak mortal; he can't do anything. I've got more raw power in my big toenail! We don't even know what's causing this fever. He's suffering from an unknown ailment that's likely going to leave him dead before he can be of any help to us. What a joke!"

"Brother Jeremy, you must control your anger. This dying man is not an ordinary human; he is the last bastion of order for a world falling rapidly into chaos."

"Yes, yes. Father, I know the scripture. I know what I saw in my visions of the future, before they were distorted and obscured by the time cancer. This is the man I was supposed to save. Well, I saved him from death by knife. Now what? Are we supposed to just let him die by whatever this is?"

"My son, have faith. Give him time. He is struggling for us; his body is fighting the Lord of Chaos as we converse. This illness is proof that he may be losing. At least, he is having a difficult time of things."

"What? He is in battle already?"

Ever patient, Father Timothy nodded. "Yes. The struggle in his body is a struggle for reality.

"Scripture states that the Lord of Chaos derives his power from an innate ability to change reality, or at least to transform our perception of reality. By inference, the one to battle the Lord of Chaos must have a similar, counteractive ability. I'm not exactly sure how it works. You and I are both all-too-well aware that much scripture is open to interpretation. However, I am certain that this ailment is further proof that the Lord of Chaos walks among us; there is a certain stink to it. I think it also confirms that this man is the one to carry us through the darkness.

"The Chaos Lord's vision for the world somehow contrasts with Petyr's vision of the world. Currently, their souls are clashing, struggling in a tournament to see whose intentions will be written into being. Petyr's will was taken by surprise; he obviously doesn't understand his powers fully, yet. There was no chance of him resisting this attack." Father Timothy sighed. "I guess we don't even really understand our own gifts. I have a feeling he will have to learn to use his abilities the same way we learned to use ours: in trial by fire."

"You mean, if he survives," Jeremy interjected. "Assuming that happens, if the Chaos Lord has already arrived then Petyr will have no chance to understand or learn to control his strength. There is no time for this. Screw it! I will go fight the Chaos Lord myself."

Father Timothy laughed. "Ha! You, a Brother of the Order of Builders, is complaining about a lack of time. Use your head, boy. The world has not been destroyed, this man hasn't expired on us, and time is still our greatest ally. You cannot fight the Lord of Chaos. It is not your fate. And face it, you wouldn't last a minute. This man, he is more like us than we are like us. His connection to Bob is at least one level above ours; he has a much tighter bond to the Lord of Order."

"But Father, those are just words. Even if what you say is true, what do they really mean?"

"What I mean is that he has access to abilities beyond our comprehension. This war with the agents of entropy is not yet lost. We must get Petyr back to health so that he can grow strong and fight for our right to exist! That is your mission. I will not allow you to throw away your life in a senseless, futile battle against the Chaos Lord. This man is our only hope now."

They turned together to observe their invalid ward. Over the course of their conversation, Petyr's writhing had diminished in intensity from the level of boa constrictor to the level of banana slug. Coincidentally, his skin was the color of an overripe banana slug; he was hardly the picture of good health.

"This poor sap is looking worse and worse," Father Timothy said. "To be totally honest, I don't think that he's going to recover on his own. He needs our help."

"What exactly are we supposed to do?" Jeremy shouted. This was too much for the young Brother to handle. "How can we help him? He's the one who is supposed to save us!"

"Jeremy, you know exactly what I must do. Don't pretend otherwise; you're not a boy anymore. Bob is ringing and I must answer His call." Father Timothy took to his feet and stretched his body out completely, relishing every stretch of his muscles. He patted his young disciple on the head. "Don't be upset with him when he wakes; he will need your support if the world is ever going to breathe easily again."

The old monk lay on the bed next to Petyr and clasped his hand; he beckoned Jeremy closer and grabbed his disciple by the hood.

"I thank you sincerely, my son. I will be waiting with open arms when Bob calls you home. Though it will probably, hopefully, be a long, long time and I will miss you. Stay safe and strong. May Bob watch over you."

Timothy closed his eyes and took a deep breath, savoring the feeling of every last molecule as it passed through his nose, his throat, his lungs, his blood, his brain. His body exhaled due to its muscular conditioning, but the monk was dead before the air left his body.

Petyr sat up, eyes darting wildly around the room. He scrambled out of bed and fell flat on his face. His complexion had already returned to a normal, healthy pink.

"My gun! Where's my gun? Look out for those shadows. They'll devour you whole!" The reality of the situation slowly crept into his eyes. No shadows, no aliens, no threat existed in the room. "Did you see any of that? Did I just hallucinate all that destruction? I just saw the world end, Jeremy!

What does that mean? I swear, it was so real. I could have sworn I was living the apocalypse."

Jeremy didn't respond immediately; his eyes were full of tears. His throat was stuffed with wails that wouldn't shake loose.

"Um, is everything okay?" Petyr asked. "Would you tell me what actually happened just now?"

Jeremy lifted a single finger and pointed at the corpse of Father Timothy, whose body had become the color of coffee-stained teeth.

Despite being healthy in body, Petyr felt terribly ill. "Oh shit."

Finally, words worked their way through Jeremy's salty mouth. "He saved you. You were gravely ill, sickened by an attack from the Chaos Lord. Father Timothy gave you his remaining time in that body and now he has returned to Bob."

Petyr's jaw dropped. He felt stun and shame spiral like a drill through his core. "But why? Why would he save me?"

Jeremy calmly stood and grabbed Petyr's wrist. "Don't you get it? You're going to stop the end of the world. You're going to stop your vision from coming to pass. Come on. You have some reality to protect."

Kosher

The turquoise waters around Figment Island bubbled furiously. The ocean maintained the perfect temperature for swimming, though being submerged felt like bathing in a tub of Perrier. The effervescence was not the result of a boiling temperature; another less tangible effect was in play.

The island's typically pristine, white beaches were littered with articles of clothing, shed by their owners like peels from oranges. The naked fruits splashed in the water, soaking up the transformative effects of the fizzy, catalytic waves. Five buoyant siblings cleansed themselves of sin and worry; they knew the arrival of their master was finally at hand. For the first time in as long as they could remember, the Figments could laugh together.

One sad peach sat alone on the shore, her fuzzy peel concealing a rotten pit.

"Come on, Ophelia! Get wet!" shouted Valkyrie. "Master will be arriving soon, you don't want to disappoint him, do you?"

"If Oedipus doesn't have to do it, I don't have to do it." Ophelia hugged her knees with resentment.

Coelacanth stopped rinsing his beard and turned toward the shore. "Don't be so ornery. Oedipus has gone missing. Lord Midas will punish her for her transgressions. She is disobeying his direct order to greet him on his arrival. You, on the other hand, are still here with us. Come into the water and bathe with your family."

"But I'm worried about Oedipus. I don't want anything to happen to her."

"Don't worry about your sister. I'm certain she is fine."

Valkyrie gargled some water and spat it into Terra's ear. "Yeah, right. That filthy pig probably got her stupid self killed doing something dumb. Ever the rebel, thinking she's better than the rest of us. Yeah, that'd be just like her."

"Ignore your sister, dear." Coelacanth splashed Valkyrie with a solid chop through the surface of the water. "We don't know what Oedipus is doing, but Master's grand entrance is nigh. Those of us present must do all we can to prepare for his arrival."

"I don't want to get undressed." Ophelia shook her head, dislodging sand that her siblings had kicked up in their rush to the sea.

Terra piped up at her remark. "Oh, just get with it, silly girl. It's fun, sis! The water feels great. Look, even Archimedes is doing it."

The lanky Science Figment pouted and crossed his arms. The noon sun blinded Ophelia as it glared off of Archimedes' pale skin.

"Ha. Ha. Ha. Ahem. You kill me, brother." Archimedes turned to his land-locked sister, his aquiline nose flaring rapidly. "Disrobe yourself, young blood. If our master is not pleased by our behavior, he might punish us or, even worse, leave us again upon arrival."

"But why do we have to do it, anyway?" Ophelia protested. "Does he really care that I bathe myself here and now? With no clothes? In these waters?"

"Ophelia!" Coelacanth's tone was unusually serious. "Don't ask such a foolish question. That's no different from asking whether or not the Master cares at all! Of course he cares. If he didn't, why would he bother to speak to you every day and every night? Why would he make the effort to imbue you with his holy wisdom? Why would he give us this land of our own and powers to complement his holiness?

"Does he really care? Ha! Come in and join us already, Ophelia. This may be the most important thing you have ever done. Do you realize that? Your role is vital. Our Master, He loves you most of all."

Valkyrie grimaced. "It's true, you ungrateful wretch. He's probably not going to appear until you get yourself wet and clean for him. Terra, come on. I think she needs some more encouragement."

The two naked siblings dashed out from the sea and pounced on their sister before she could rise to her feet. Valkyrie held struggling Ophelia down on the sand while Terra aggressively removed her clothing. Ophelia's siblings grinned at her futile attempts to escape, feeble kicks and spineless bites; she squealed with fury, but her noises only encouraged her siblings to play rougher. Together they picked the newly naked Ophelia up and returned to the sea. Valkyrie grabbed her sister's head and forced it under a coming wave.

As the briny current swept over her body and mind, Ophelia felt relieved. A quick gulp of the water filled her with its transformative magic. She immediately understood the necessity for her ecdysis; a metamorphosis was underway and the clothing only got in the way. As the dirt on her skin eroded, her feelings of dread were swept away by the riptide. She floated to the surface with a smile on her face. Her Master was coming at long last!

The bubbling in the water increased tenfold; the earth beneath the ocean tenaciously trembled. A monstrous wave appeared on the horizon's edge, its peak capped with frothy excitement. The six Figments floated and watched calmly as the tsunami ambled toward them relentlessly. They offered no resistance as it picked them up and carried them like tiny burrs stuck in its socks. The

122

wave finally broke halfway across the island, spilling the Figments onto a grassy knoll immediately north of the Castle Figment.

Proudly standing at the center of the hill was King Midas, Figment of Creation, Lord of Chaos.

His highness' figure was far from the image Ophelia had conjured in her head. Before her stood a small boy, as scrawny and bony as he was confident. The only truly imposing thing about young Midas' visage was a pair of mooselike, crystalline antlers growing out of his head, behind a pair of exaggerated ears. The antlers mangled any light that passed over his head, focusing and splintering it in a wild spectrum of colors wherever he chose to turn his head.

The Figments lay sprawled around the knoll, propping themselves up on their naked elbows to look upon their risen messiah. Six jaws hung slack, attached to faces composed of infinitely permuting disbelief. The Figment siblings could not believe that the coming of their Lord had finally occurred. It seemed even more improbable that he would turn out to be a young boy instead of the noble king that they had been promised. The all-mighty Father of Chaos wasn't even old enough to procreate.

"This is some serious bull," Valkyrie rose to her feet. Her brow was furrowed like a heavily irrigated plain. "You aren't the Creation Figment. You can't possibly be the Father of Chaos. What in hell's ashes is a little boy going to do to destroy this world?"

The young king turned towards his insubordinate daughter. He didn't speak a word but furrowed his brow right back. The other Figments watched the stare-down with baited breath, feeling awkward tension vibrate through the air.

The crystal antlers started to glow as though some hidden generator had suddenly switched on to fill them with power. As Midas concentrated harder, the glow transferred itself down through his body, deeper and deeper into his corporal form.

He leaped into the air, halting his ascent immediately before Valkyrie's stubborn face. He balled his childish hands into tight little fists and smashed them both into Valkyrie's cheeks with an explosive flash. All the energy from the trapped light coursed through his body like it was a conduction rod, blasting Valkyrie with every mote of power the young king could muster. She flew backwards, floating gracefully until her body crashed into a tree growing at the bottom of the knoll. She was knocked unconscious by the impact, lying cold with no more than a twitch for several minutes.

Midas turned back to his other children.

"Come on, y'all. Y'all are lookin' at me like I'm some kinda inbred freak. It's me, Midas!" The boy threw his head about wildly, covering his fellow

Figments in rainbow auras. "Hey, ya want me to sing and dance about it? Do ya?

"Ah, of course, my Lord." A bright red flush took to Coelacanth's cheeks, turning his beard a frivolous pink. "Please forgive our rudeness. We were all but toddlers on our arrival. How could we expect the Master of Chaos to be fully-grown and in full strength? Your advanced stage of growth should be seen as inspiring."

"Yeah, sure." The boy king's voice lacked the confidence of his pose. "That's probably exactly it, Pops."

The newborn king looked around at his domain as though he had never glimpsed it before. "Hey, this island is pretty nice, right? Been a good home for y'all?"

Silent nods passed around the circle. Valkyrie moaned incoherently from the bottom of the knoll.

"Well, good. Enjoy it while ya can. We're leavin' as soon as I'm at full strength. Maybe two, three days tops. Then I'm gonna melt this whole place into the sea, so nobody else can ever call it home. How's that sound?" Midas continued without waiting for response. "Then, we're gonna start our march through the universe, bringin' the glory of entropy to all the nonbelievers. I figure we start with the human planet, to reward them for all the help they've been in bringin' me back to existence."

A trace of worry slipped over Midas face. "Hold up. There're supposed to be seven of y'all, right? Why am I only countin' six? Someone think they're too important to greet me?"

The Figments looked around, sharing nervous glances amongst themselves. None among them wanted to sell out their old sister or ire their young brother. Ophelia finally managed the courage to speak up.

"Well, sir. It's Oedipus, sir. She's been missing for several days now. Nobody knows where she's gotten to, uh, sir."

"Okay. Thank you, dear, I knew there was I reason I chose you as my favorite. So honest and pure. And pretty, too. Well, I gotta get used to the new body, right? Gotta give it an easy test to start, yeah? I'm a' goin' to kill that stupid ingrate sister of yours, first chance I get!

"Oh, but I'm gettin' ahead of myself. First things first. Someone's gotta take me to see my castle and make me some grub. Ophelia, I choose you."

While Coelacanth and Ophelia led Midas to the Castle Figment throne room, the other Figments lagged behind to help Valkyrie regain her footing.

"So," Lazarus murmured, "First impressions of the new boss?"

Valkyrie struggled to speak through her swollen cheeks. "Mmph. Hmmmmm."

"Yes, yes. I figured you would say something like that. You just focus on staying upright and leave the talking to us for now."

"You know," Terra started, "I was just a little bit underwhelmed. I mean, our Lord and Master hasn't even hit puberty yet. Sure he can pack a punch, but if our poor sister hadn't been caught off guard it would probably be him we're carrying. Or, rather, trying to carry. Would you quit being a baby, dear sister?"

Archimedes stood off to the side as his brothers struggled to lift their heaviest sister off the ground. "I must concur. Something is wrong; things are not going according to his plans. If everything were as it should be, we would have met a much different man. In fact, the universe would probably already be burning away to nothingness."

"How do you mean?" Lazarus asked. "The stage was set for his arrival. Would he have come if it were not the time for him to start his reign?"

"I have a hypothesis that those monks you all slaughtered weren't the real problem preventing our master's arrival. And yes, I know it was you idiots who did that silliness, don't pretend you thought I wouldn't notice. I think something much more sinister and subtle is at play; those Brothers of Order were merely the stick ends that we could see poking up on the surface of a very deep bog. "

      "I think," Lazarus mused, "That, for once, I really wish I knew what our absent sister was thinking."

lozenge

The calm before a storm only appears serene through hindsight. Before lightning strikes, soldiers keep on fighting, workers keep on toiling, and dreamers keep on praying, The hustling, bustling world waits for no man, beast, or flora. And so it goes and on and on up until the moment when the biggest meteor crashes through orbit, the first cow gets picked up by ferocious winds, and the last Mohican rides into the setting sun.

The Minotaur had a secret tell to warn him when a storm was brewing: the deepest part of his throat would break out in a colony of hives. He had been compulsively popping soothing lozenges for the last several days; his world was undergoing some drastic changes, mostly for the worse.

Ever since that miserable excuse for a secret agent had given his name up to the Dom Com and quit Anonymous, the Minotaur's carefully constructed labyrinth had begun dissolving into bitter little crumbs.

Rumors spread quickly though the hordes of henchmen employed by Minotaur Corp. Some whispered that the disloyal Russian agent had given up information on the headquarters and operations to save his own skin, betraying his former compatriots. Others claimed he had been a turncoat all along and had only let himself get caught because he enjoyed the sensations of torture. The most disturbing rumors involved the spy creating his own team of players to compete in the game against his old boss. The Minotaur took another lozenge and popped it into his mouth. Cherry flavor.

The moist healing aura of the pill coated his mouth and swept down his throat. The medicine had such a delightful, comforting flavor. The Minotaur chuckled; it was too funny that the center of a delectable cherry's pit was filled with noxious cyanide.

Sucking fervently, the Minotaur paced about his living room. All of the rumors had been revealed to be little more than poorly constructed libel. There was no point in him worrying about such ancient problems.

The game Anonymous was over, after all. He had lost the fight for power; his quest for the betterment of the world was officially over. He needed to face the facts and get on with his life. Minotaur Corp was slowly disbanding. His henchmen were scattering themselves to the far corners of the earth. He had taken the opportunity to retreat to his Mediterranean island home. Minos Island was known to be secluded and safe, a sanctuary for his body and mind.

Despite his careful distribution of resources and effective micromanagement, the Minotaur just couldn't muster enough chaos to be crowned Most Entropic Villain. No, that honor was bestowed to his most prolific rival, the Epitaph.

Just the thought of that turtlehead brought an acute tightness to his throat, so the Minotaur swallowed another lozenge from his bag. This time he grabbed mango, his favorite flavor. Such a transportational sweetness, no other fruit could compare. However, the plant was a member of the sumac family; it was a distant relative of poison ivy. While the flesh of the fruit was undeniably tasty, the peel could cause severe allergic reactions ranging from rashes to death. Delicious irony carried the Minotaur away from his stressful state of mind to a place of tranquil logic.

A formal announcement had swept through the major e-media outlets three days ago.

"Descending Hegemon Names Successor and Abdicates Office!" read the headlines

"Watch The Rising Star of Hegemon Epitaph!"

"Hegemon Solomon R.I.P."

The Hegemon had abdicated without a struggle? He simply walked away from his duty, filling the power vacuum with a hand-picked successor?

Inconceivable! And yet, it was true.

Illness was the reason Hegemon Solomon gave for ceding his throne. He claimed that the disease had spread so far and so quickly that his judgment had become flawed and his mind ineffectual. The land's new ruler, Hegemon Epitaph, had been a secret disciple of the Hegemony for years. She had been vetted for the position of world leader, well trained in Solomon's policies so she could continue to make appropriate decisions to better the world.

Every single word was a lie, but the Hegemon spoke them such that every member of the unkempt masses should believe him and have faith in the system. After all, at the end of the day, that was what he did for a living.

Adverse pundits wasted no time in writing their dissenting opinions. Later that day, after the initial shock of the news had worn off, a second wave of articles cluttered the press sites.

"The Epitaph to Give Society's Eulogy?"

"No Votes Allowed! When Did We Learn Despotism?"

"Show Your Face! Don't Be Led By an Invisible Leash!"

"Administration Reanimated as Bunch of Zombies?"

Every personality on the internet suddenly constructed an opinion about the state of world politics. Forums exploded, polarized by the government's paradigm shift. Hegemony related memes sprang up like weeds after a rainstorm.

Opinions were strongly divided on the fate of the Hegemony and the world itself. Some bloggers ranted about how this secret leader would lead the human race to destruction; others preached blind faith in the Hegemony and death to all who oppose her rule. A small percent claimed that everything was an elaborate hoax to distract humans from the real enemies, awakening Atlantean vampires.

Chaos loomed beyond every hyperlink. Brothers wrote against brothers; mind tapped against mind. Less than one day into her office, the Epitaph had accidentally incited a virtual civil war.

And yet, all of the zealots managed to miss the smaller, more important picture. Nobody cared about the machinations of Anonymous. The game and its players were still secret to the greater portion of the world's population. None of the ignorant citizens understood that this chaos, this divisive entropy pulling the world apart, was the ultimate prize for the game all along. The Minotaur knew and it sickened him to see the human race used for such a device.

Not one person outside the game knew that the Hegemon was abdicating purely out of fear.

Though every player in Anonymous was scary in their own way, none of them compared to the invisible Figments. The old Hegemon was only human; he could be coerced as easily as a child. Abdication under duress is not a foreign concept to the realm of realpolitik. If the Figments had truly planned this game with the intent of leading the world to civil war, the fear they could potentially instill in the heart of one man was beyond reason.

The Epitaph had proven herself worthy of a throne that governed through terror's fist. Hopefully, she was brave enough to continue sitting on it. Otherwise, the Minotaur feared, the Figments might continue with a more devious endeavor to further the production of Chaos.

A loud pounding at his front door interrupted the Minotaur's meditations; it rattled the windows as well as his brain. Still tipsy with a bit of shock, he took a glance out the peephole before deciding whether or not to open the door.

A giant, surly man was standing at his doorstep with a large package gripped between his massive hamfists.

"Who is this?" asked the Minotaur.

"S'cuse me. Hello? Package for the Minotaur, sah."

A lurking paranoia tapped on the Minotaur's shoulder. "Ah, yes. Just leave it, thank you. I've lost my pants at the moment, hmm, and all the others are dirty."

"Nope. The Hippo needs to ensure delivery, sah. Not leavin' 'til the Hippo gets it."

That name rang a bell in the Minotaur's steeple. The stranger's manner of speaking was punctuated by ill will. Something didn't feel right. Minos Island was his secret hideaway, an island he had bought decades ago. As a young man, the Minotaur had dreamed of forging a new world order. He planned to rule the planet from this tiny Mediterranean paradise, his fortress of solitude, far away from any enemies that might wish him ill.

Now he was old and withered, living on the island to escape from his foes. He had certainly caused a ruckus during his tenure as an Anonymous player. But had any of it really mattered? The Epitaph now gripped the reins of the world; it was she who would make the decisions remembered by the history books. The Minotaur was a washed up old villain; he'd been in the chaos business so long he couldn't even remember his original name.

The Minotaur popped another lozenge before his throat reignited from worry. The flavor was lemon, another ironic fruit. The incredibly intense flavor distracted lemon-eaters from the nature of the acids that gave the fruit such sourness. Bite after bite, it was more and more addicting. However, with every drop of juice more flesh was burned away.

"Okay. Just give me a second." The Minotaur dashed upstairs and grabbed the gun hidden underneath his silk lined pillow. With one third of life spent in the sack, he had tried to keep it as comfortable as possible. He bounded back down the stairs, taking care to make as much noise as possible.

He opened the front door and his unexpected guest thrust the large package at him. The Minotaur juggled it, nearly dropping it onto his toes; it was a lot heavier than he expected.

"Open it now, sah. Right here is fine. It's important."

The Minotaur forced a pained smile. "Ah. Yes. Of course." He cautiously slit open the edges of the big, brown package.

Inside the box was a marble statue of Hermes. He was posed in a traditional fashion, dashing into the future. The detail on the statue was incredible. The artist had depicted everything perfectly, from the winged shoes to the crease of his brow. In his right hand, extended before him, was an envelope inlayed with gold script that read: *To My Worthy Adversary.*

There was only one person who would have the gall and resources to send this present to his private island, his secret lair: the parcel was from the damn Hegemon.

He took the envelope gingerly, rubbing the gold fleur de lis with his thumb. It remained undisturbed; it was made from the genuine article, pure metal inlaid on paper. He took out the card inside and read it to himself.

Dear Minotaur,

No hard feelings, okay?

You fought well, but the battle was hard and frankly, stacked against you. I'm the victor but my fight is just beginning. I wish to make you an offer to soothe the burning you must be feeling. A salve for your ego, if you will.

I want you to come join me in my efforts to bring about a new order of chaos. I think a Minister position would be just right for you. Perhaps, the Finance Minister? I know how much you love that cash. Give your answer to my emissary.

Sincerely,

The Epitaph

The Minotaur's eyes widened. The gall of that woman!

"Really? Does she actually expect me to accept this invitation to her little party? What if I don't accept? What will she do? Do I even have a choice?" The irritations deep in the Minotaur's throat began to swell again.

He popped another lozenge, a pineapple flavor washed over his tongue. The taste reminded him of jackfruit, one of the most dangerous fruits of the world. The jackfruit tree was known to kill many an unwary pedestrian as they walked beneath its branches. Its fruit could grow as large as eighty pounds, enough to crush an oblivious skull passing underneath when it ripened and fell from its branch.

"Now, sah, there's always a choice. 'S just that ya might not like your options. The Epitaph ordered the Hippo to deliver similar invitations to all the major players. If ya don't take the position, somebody else will. At that point, ya become unnecessary and the Hippo has to give ya another, harder present."

The Minotaur saw through the Epitaph's actions immediately. The current bureaucracy would never truly accept her as ruler of the known world. Her back-story was just too bizarre, appearing on the political scene just as the former Hegemon announced he was leaving. She was a wild card, mysterious and frightening.

So, she was going to bypass the entire bureaucracy. The current system, set up by Hegemon Solomon, would remain in place for appearances only. Her plan for administration was to run the show via Epitaph Industries until the whole world truly believed she was its master. The virtual civil war would give her the perfect opportunity to set up a healthy government while opposing minds were distracted by battle.

No doubt she wanted to bring her enemies as close as possible. While her face was becoming public, she needed to make sure machinations remained invisible and anonymous.

"This is obscene. There's no way she can pull this off. It's unthinkable."

"Okay, if ya say so." The Hippo shrugged. "So, what's it gonna be, sah?"

The Minotaur needed to think fast. He snapped up another lozenge, but immediately spat it onto the ground. Grape. A weak, little fruit, it grew sweeter as it withered away with age. He hated grapes; they reminded him of his own fermentation. The candy was only in his mouth for a second, but the flavor would remain for hours to come.

Grimacing, the Minotaur gave his reply. "Fine. You've got me. I'll march along with the Epitaph's feeble parade, for now. Let me pack my things."

Menagerie

Exactly one week passed between Midas' arrival and Oedipus' return to Figment Island. It had also been a week since Oedipus' inauguration as Hegemon of the human realm.

Oedipus knew something had changed from the moment her foot hit the white tiled floor. An aura in the air was different; the way the molecules moved or the way she moved through them was wrong. It felt as though someone had reversed the magnetic field, flipping the polarity of the environment.

She snuck out of Archimedes' labs and walked calmly towards her quarters. The best defense in this situation was no defense. The more natural she appeared, the less suspicious her siblings would be.

Everything went smoothly until she reached Figment Hall, the dining chamber of Castle Figment. She heard a commotion and decided to step inside to greet her kin. It would be better to come clean to her family members about her return than to let them discover her actions on their own. However, her family did not await her in the Hall.

A long table was lined with enough food to quarter an army, but only one person was eating.

He was emphatically, methodically devouring every culinary delight within his arms' reach. Great crystalline antlers grew from his head, long and slender like a reindeer's adornments. This young man was a stranger to Oedipus, yet she knew exactly whom she had stumbled upon.

"So, when did you get in?" Oedipus asked. "I'm sorry I wasn't here to greet you, Lord Midas."

Midas chewed his meat thoughtfully before responding. "That's all right, Oed. I know you've got important business with important folks. If you can't make time to spend with your dear old dad after eons of separation, I understand." His words were lathered with a coat of cold irony, so subtle that Oedipus almost believed him. "I got in about a week ago. It's probably best you weren't here, I was embarrassingly out of shape, you know. But now I'm as fit as a button, ready to go spread some disarray!"

Oedipus smiled nervously. "I'm so glad to hear it. Took you long enough to get here, though. This universe has had more than its share of organization and order."

The King wagged his finger at his daughter's wild tongue. "Oh, ho ho, Oed. Watch yourself, dear. You're just as sharp as I remember you, from when I was speaking with you from beyond the sea. That feels like forever ago, am I right?"

"Yeah, it does. I've got to admit, I was pretty happy when you stopped spewing your righteous babble into my ears and started squawking at my little brother instead."

"Well, you know, it was to be anticipated. The youngest are always the closest to their parents, after all. I shouldn't have expected you to be my willing vessel forever. Some of your siblings were a bit more enthusiastic about staying in touch with me. You might have forced me onto Terra, but he tried to hard to keep me in his heart. He wanted to deprive Ophelia of her time with me. Oh, speaking of your sister...Ophelia, attend to me."

Ophelia appeared immediately from behind Midas' chair. Oedipus was surprised. Had she been sitting there the whole time the King was eating? Even more disturbing was the look on her face, a limpid frown, distanced from true emotion. She met Oedipus's eyes with her own for a brief second, but quickly turned them down to the floor.

"Yes, my lord. How may I serve you?"

"Ah, dear. Clean this mess." Midas gestured at the table, still covered with freshly prepared, entirely edible food. "I need no speak with your sister about some very important things. Just take this away and start preparing my dinner. I plan on working up quite the appetite this afternoon."

Midas rose from his chair and released a satisfied sigh. "Well, Oed, I'm stuffed. Let's walk and talk."

Oedipus walked just behind Midas as he led her toward a massive door with a complex locking mechanism stretched across it. A convoluted series of wires and bars were woven into a protective tapestry; Oedipus couldn't even imagine how to start dismantling the seal. Next to the door was a gridded pad, with various squares lit up in different colors.

Midas started playing with the pad, seemingly randomly. He flicked different squares and the pattern of lights changed until they all glowed light green.

"Funny news from the world outside, eh?" Midas said, "Somebody finally won that silly game I concocted! On the same day that I arrived? I guess I'm pretty smart, after all, hmm? Tricked the humans into bringing about their own destruction?"

"Yeah, it's pretty funny, I guess." Oedipus couldn't tell how much information the King had obtained from the world or whether he knew her secret agenda. His voice wasn't giving away any clues.

"Yeah, but you know the real joke, don't you? It's on that newly crowned Hegemon," Midas chuckled as he continued to play with the keypad. "That poor sap just sat on his ill-gotten throne and we're gonna steal his kingdom out from underneath him. Can you imagine? Less than a month in office and the world gets destroyed. Worst Hegemon ever!"

Oedipus heart sunk until it should have pumping on the ground. She had no idea whether Midas was hinting at her destruction, but signs were pointing to a bitter Master. It was probably safest just to play along and humor him for now.

Something clicked in the door and the keypad emitted a tiny victory tone. The locking mechanism began to untangle itself, seemingly on a will of its own. A dark, stinky air whiffed into the Hall as the door opened backwards into darkness. Flickering lights illuminated a spiral staircase poorly. Oedipus looked back to Midas, only to find the King staring at her with an asphyxiating intensity.

"Well," he said, "Let's give you a tour."

Oedipus had never seen this part of the castle before this trip underground. As far as she could remember, there had never been a descending stairwell in the northwest corner of Figment Hall. Someone had done some very efficient remodeling since she'd been gone. First, she'd found her sister, owned like a slave, and now this. She wondered what others changes had occurred in her absence.

During the descent, Midas talked incessantly about his time asleep and the grandiose vision he had for the world. Oedipus let his words wash through her ears without absorbing any of them. He had tried to talk to her like this before, when she was his vessel, and she hadn't paid him any attention then, either.

"You see," Midas continued, "While I was sleeping I never stopped dreaming. I dreamed of fire and water, of earth and ice, and, most frequently, of hideous beasts."

As the duo reached the bottom of the stairs, a terrible screech cut through the air and a tiny demon appeared, dropping from the ceiling. It had a rooster's body supported by eight, hairy spider-legs. The creature scuttled about erratically, springing into the air and flapping its wings furiously in an attempt to stay afloat. Oedipus was unsure if it was attacking or attempting to escape, but the sticky liquid it left in its wake suggested the latter.

Midas clasped his hands together and held them at his chest. He tensed all the muscles in his torso, squeezing something between his hands. The spider-cock disappeared with a muffled puff. The sticky substance remained, staining the walls of the passage with putrid ectoplasm.

"Pardon me, sometimes I forget to lock these bastards up. Or, maybe they just find their way out and about."

The Creation Figment gestured that they should continue walking. Oedipus followed his command, unable to resist. She remained silent as he continued his egomaniacal monologue.

"Now that I have awakened once more, I am literally bringing my dreams to life. Growing my subconscious goals to the point of fruition. These creatures have marinated in my mind for a long while and now they shall see the light of day, before I snuff it out forever. I am rapidly rediscovering my skills, conjuring these nightmarish phages to plague the world of men. Every day with each successful summoning, I grow a little bit closer to my full potential."

Midas took his daughter's trembling hand in a firm grip and escorted her deeper into the dungeon. Oedipus peered into the darkness of the cells beside her as she walked, trying to stay as close to the center of the path as she could.

Behind magically reinforced glass, strange chimeras met her frightened stares with eyes made from flames far colder than ice. Their bodies were misshapen and their minds were more crooked than a matchstick man. A great, muscular bear with the head of a parrot was singing a wordless melody as its limbs shifted up and down its body.

A winged scorpion attacked the walls of its cell with three of its four tails. The fourth tail might have joined in, but it was too busy attacking the scorpion hawk's cellmate, a flying frog that occasionally burped laser blasts.

"As you can see, I have a veritable menagerie of terror that I will unleash as our honor guard. They will precede our march into the mortal realm and give the humans of earth a chance to truly understand that their time is running thin. Nothing will stop our legion of horrors.

"But, come a little further, my daughter," Midas said, smiling devilishly. "I've almost finished something that has got me truly proud of myself."

Oedipus could no longer keep track of how far they had traveled. Part of her mind tried to divine their current position. All her instincts put their location somewhere deep beneath the ocean, but no leaks had appeared and no sounds of waves crept through the subterranean walls. As she and Midas traveled deeper into the dungeon, the terrors grew more and more abstract and horrific.

Several cells down from the scorpion fly, Oedipus saw a cloud of dust trapped exceptionally thick glass Parts of the cloud would spontaneously condense into levitating rocks. As she stared, the cloud polymorphed into fifty small stones that began to click together menacingly.

The cell across from the dust devil appeared to be empty. As Oedipus took a closer look inside, she could see patterns of the back wall shifting and rearranging themselves. She had no idea what could

147

be causing it to happen and decided that she would be better off remaining ignorant.

Finally, Midas stopped his advance. They had reached a small wooden door, half as tall as Oedipus. It was slightly decrepit, starting to disintegrate; it didn't look like it could have contained any of the other monstrosities from the dungeon. Most of them could have burst through it or effervesced through its cracks.

"Take a look inside," Midas offered. "I promise, it won't bite."

Oedipus shook her head. "I'm all right. It's the other things it might do that have me more concerned."

Midas grabbed her hand once more, a quiet rage strengthening his grip. "Really, I insist."

With one last look into Oedipus' shock widened eyes, he opened the door and flung his daughter through the threshold. She hit her head on the top of the threshold and passed out immediately. Her body slid a short distance and vanished into the darkness, beyond the reach of salvation or even hope.

"Noxious," Midas called, "Come here! I've got a treat for my favorite girl."

Midas quickly shut the door once more. He had worked too hard to create this phantasm; he would take no chances that it might escape. There

148

was a special function it still needed to fulfill. Midas was particularly proud of this creation. Finally he was a little bit scared for his own safety.

Listening at the door, Midas could hear a tearing sound. He could smell the stench of entropic flow; sickly sweet and pungent, all at once.

"That's a good girl. There's plenty more where that came from."

The newly crowned Hegemon sat up sharply in her bed. The memories had flooded her so subtly she had thought them a dream. She knew better; this had all been part of the plan.

The Hegemon rolled out of bed and slipped her feet into the warm, snug cozies that awaited them. Her black-and-white silk pajamas clung delicately to her warm glowing skin. The memories were still trickling in.

Her double's personality seamlessly slipped into her own. It was easy enough, when planned ahead of time. Because she and her clone had so completely agreed with each other, they had already shared each other's mind and heart. Now, they shared one body.

She doubted the Good Doctor would ever feel at ease in his mind again. Twelve angry souls fighting for dominance over one body would never come to terms with each other. He was doomed to have a fractured mind until death.

Oedipus would have pitied him, but he made such a useful tool in his current state. Once her plan was in motion, he wouldn't have to suffer much longer.

Yawning, Oedipus shuffled over to her dresser and picked up her phone. Without hesitation, she entered a text that she had been itching to send for days.

H - THE TROUT IS HOOKED. BEGIN REELING IT IN – E

In a perfect world, the Hippo would get the message and begin phase two of her master plan immediately. Tomorrow, she would wake up with her problems solved and her life a blank slate. Of course, this wasn't a perfect world, but a girl could dream.

If everything continued as she hoped, there would be no need for a Figment King, a Hegemon, or a war between Chaos and Order. Oedipus smiled as she lay back down in her four-post bed and snuggled herself beneath the satin covers. For the moment, she would try to enjoy every bit of pleasure she could grasp; every savory breath could wind up being her last.

Nascence

"Think back," Jeremy said, "Throughout your entire life. Has there ever been a moment when something happened that you couldn't explain rationally?"

Petyr groaned. "No. No. No. We've been over this so many times already. I've never had anything truly inexplicable or extraordinary happen to me. I've never felt like I had a special ability. I've never been touched by magic. Trust me, I've never been anything more than a plain, old secret agent. And now, I'm just a washed up agent, even more spectacular than before."

"There's no need to be upset, Petyr," Jeremy said, "We need to discover your innate ability somehow, and this is the easiest way. Most probably."

"Look," Petyr said, "We've skimmed through just about every sacred text you and your brothers had hidden away. I've practically told you my life story. I just don't think that we're going to figure this out. If I'm going to do this, I'm better off going and fighting this bastard the way I work best: with a gun. Hopefully, my ability or whatever will manifest itself in time to save me."

"No. That's not an option of acceptable risk. You saw the shadows during your fever, there's no stopping them with guns alone," Jeremy sighed. Working with Petyr always left him quite exhausted, but he had to try hard, for Timothy's sake. "Look, I know we haven't had much success recently, so we're going to try something a little bit different today.

"I've brewed some tea I found in Brother Bartholomew's secret stash. Ascending Phoenix, Monkey-Picked, Green Pearls. I think he would approve of us borrowing it, may Bob watch over his soul. It's a special blend that he used for meditation, so I though we could try to use it and tap into your subconscious."

"Fine, I'll give it a shot." Petyr grabbed one of the hot mugs and started drinking, diligently. "I don't know what my subconscious could tell me that my conscious couldn't. Oh! Bleargh," he gagged. "Did you wash this mug? This tea tastes kinda funny. Tasts lirk. Urg."

Jeremy caught Petyr's head as the secret agent fell under the tea's sway. He held the heavy skull in his lap and stroked his friend's dark locks.

"It's okay, just breathe deeply, Petyr. Breathe deep and easy."

When Petyr opened his eyes, he found himself in the midst of a thick jungle's breadth. The

152

sky was almost completely blocked by a mosaic canopy, a tight weave of intertwined leaves and vines. An emerald mist formed a thin slipcover on the underbrush, swirling and churning as tiny creatures skittered beneath it.

A faint chittering drew Petyr's attention to a tree behind him. Sitting on the lowest branch of the tree, a small lemur voraciously gnawed on something that refused to quit wriggling. Petyr couldn't tell if the feast was a worm or a snake, but the lemur was certainly savoring its flavor.

The lemur suddenly noticed his silent human companion and stopped his furious mastication. The beast held out the writhing mass in his hand, making an offering to the stranger who had stumbled into his home. He stared at Petyr with full, dark pupils, while chattering and chawing like a raving lunatic. Unsure of how to respond, Petyr received the gift gratefully. Upon closer inspection, he realized that the snake-like snack was actually a strange looking millipede.

The Lemur clenched his fists and made an eating gesture; he wanted his new friend to understand the great joy he had found hidden within the insect's body. Petyr complied; he cautiously brought the millipede closer to his mouth. Its carapace was orange with black stripes, an obvious warning to predators. Despite a growing unease in his stomach, Petyr trusted his deranged prosimian companion. He put one end of the millipede into his mouth and gently massaged it, testing the waters gently.

As soon as his teeth touched the insect's shell, it emitted a low hissing noise. A warm, viscous liquid leaked from the many-legged creature onto his tongue, tasting vaguely of almonds.

Within seconds, Petyr's vision began to tunnel and he felt himself rise above the forest's ceiling. Without understanding why, Petyr knew he could fly wherever he wished. He could see that he was floating in a large basin with canopy stretching up and over its lips. Determined to explore the region further, Petyr swiftly glided along the treetops, spying on the forest's oblivious denizens as they went about their animal business. As he burst out of the valley, a vast grassland expanded before his eyes, shrinking off into an infinite horizon. The forest died away almost immediately at the top of the valley, until only a few sparse groves spotted the plains.

A wild river escaped from the forest not twenty feet from where Petyr hovered. It appeared to be flowing against the pull of gravity, up and out of the basin. Petyr allowed himself to fall just above the surface of the river before speeding along its flowing waters.

He could clearly see his reflection staring back from a nightmare land under the water; his eyes appeared pitch black, somehow hollowed during his travels. Petyr reached out to touch himself, but only succeeded in shattering his face into one thousand tiny spirals.

As Petyr zoomed along the river, an image appeared that was not a mirror of his present. He could see his reflected self, bound to a dungeon wall. He knew this scene; he had experienced it once before, when he was captured by the Dom Com. He saw her speaking to him; he felt himself being tortured yet again. But just before he would renounce his eligibility to play the game, the river split in two.

Rather than stop his flight or choose one path to follow, Petyr took a simpler approach and split himself in two. Each body flew down its own branch of the river, watching a drama unfold beneath the river's surface.

The Petyr to the east watched as he gave his true name and disqualified himself from playing Anonymous; the Petyr to the west saw himself resist, remaining incarcerated and tortured for a very long time.

Both rivers split once more and Petyr divided along with them. Four washed up agents swept down the flood plains. One Petyr saw himself released, escaping into an unfamiliar world where his enemies deigned to hunt him down. Another Petyr saw himself slowly realize a love for the Dom Com, falling victim to Stockholm Syndrome. The third Petyr saw himself shot by an assassin only a few days after his escape. The last Petyr was killed in an overzealous torture session. These last two rivers ended suddenly, collecting in small puddles on the grassy flats. The Petyr clones that had been following these paths dove into the puddles, never to emerge.

The other rivers split, on and on and on. Paths split, over and over as more potential storylines revealed themselves. As new branches were born, Petyr kept multiplying himself to follow them all. This effect repeated itself, over and over, until the flood plains were no longer any part land. The multitude of rivulets had bifurcated so many times they overlapped with one another, creating a homogenous blend of all possible paths. The river had finally reached its end point, the ocean.

Looking at the unfathomable mass of water and timelines was too difficult for Petyr's human brain to handle. An infinite number of possibilities awaited him in this depthless abyss. The mere idea of following any of them any further, splitting himself to infinity, startled him and brought on a sense of panic. This wilderness was unreal; Petyr wanted desperately to escape.

He and his hundred billion brothers turned from the ocean and began a rapid ascent. The vision of infinite possibility would not leave his mind's eye; it was seared there as though a brand had been placed in his center of his vision. The only way he could possibly forget it and think clearly again was to purge the thought forcefully. Like a school of minnows, the fleet of Petyr's turned sharply, their path now aimed directly at the largest star in the sky, the sun. Faster and faster they flew, locked in a great race. Each wanted to forget this terrifying sight as quickly as he was able.

When the fleet of clones was approximately one light year from the sun, an improbable horror happened. A great visage appeared on the sun. It belonged to a man with eyes impeccably stern. His features were as perfect as a model's, but great fiery antlers erupted from his skull.

It was too late for the Petyr regatta to stop; their momentum was too great. The fiery face opened its mouth as wide as possible; one hundred billion copies of Petyr Dmitriev haphazardly flew into the gaping maw.

One iteration of Petyr was able to stop himself; somehow, he had seen this coming and decelerated just in time. He simply watched as the sun demon chewed on his temporal brethren. He saw it smile with joy at the flavors erupting from every single crunchy chew. With a mighty roar and foolhardy bravado, Petyr charged at the massive inferno.

As his tiny fist was about to connect with the gargantuan star, Petyr woke up.

"Petyr! Petyr! It's all right. You're safe."

Petyr looked directly up Jeremy's nostrils before jumping to his feet.

"What happened? What did you do to that tea?"

"Me? I didn't do anything! I swear! Granted, I've never made tea on my own, before. I may have used a bit much."

"A bit much! I was transported to another world, thank you very much!" Petyr sputtered, his mind still racing from the strange vision.

"Calm down, Petyr. You were screaming. But it's okay. You're safe now. Tell me what you saw. Let's think about it together, try and figure it out."

Petyr nodded. "Actually, I think I get it. Sort of. I don't know how, it doesn't make sense, but I get it. I know what I need to do.

"I saw myself; I watched my life as it could have happened. An infinitude of possibilities spawned other possibilities. There are so many paths my life could have taken, but didn't. I saw so many disasters I could have experienced, but I survived. For whatever reason, I am here today with you, fighting this epic evil.

"I mean, obviously, my decisions and actions have caused me to be in my current situation. But, I think there's more to it than that. I have to take back what I said earlier, about my life having no inexplicable occurrences. Looking back on my life, I did notice something strange. I have never been shot, not once, in my entire tenure as a gun-toting secret agent. I've been in a hundred gunfights and never been grazed. Doesn't that seem strange to you?"

Jeremy was perplexed. "That seems highly unusual, yes. But it doesn't strike me as impossible."

Petyr nodded. "Right. If I had been shot, my life would have changed. I would have spent time in a hospital instead of doing something else. I might have died. I might have become a cripple. But I didn't."

"Yes. Yes. What brilliant insight you have. What's your point?"

"Well, I'm wondering if I didn't have something to do with that."

Jeremy laughed. "You mean, you actually think that you chose not to get hit by any of those bullets?"

Petyr nodded, his face serious. "Yes. That's exactly what I mean. There are hundreds of ways my life could go at any second. Whether or not I get shot is a very simple example. I think I might be able to choose among all possibilities and select the one that best suits my survival."

Jeremy put a finger to his lips. "Well, yeah. Actually, that makes a lot of sense, when you put it that way. It also fits with the scripture that says your ability is supposed to counteract King Midas' ability. He's trying to destroy reality, but you are able to create it!

"This is fantastic! Oh, Father Timothy would be so happy right now. Petyr! We can do this; we can protect reality! So, do you have any idea how to use it? Is it functional?"

Petyr shook his head. "No, I don't think so. I'm pretty clueless as to how I use the power or even the extent it can protect me. It seems entirely passive at this point, but maybe it can do other things, too? If I've been using it all along, it seems like I should just let it operate on its own, right? It seems like it knows what's best for me, even better than I do."

"Well, I guess so. Just let it work things out? Well, it's not exactly the most reassuring plan, but it makes sense." Jeremy agreed. "Huh."

"What's wrong?"

"Well, before you drank the tea, you mentioned that you wanted to go take on Midas with your gun, the way you best know how to handle things. It seems like you may have been right after all."

Petyr smiled. "Well, that suits me just fine. I'll just treat this like my old job. One more special mission never hurt anybody, right? Come on, friend, we have some reality to defend."

Obtuse

"Thank you for gathering so efficiently, on such short notice. I know you are all eager to discuss the issues facing us in these dark days, but please give me a brief moment. We are having a technical difficulty."

The Hegemon's first official press conference had barely begun and was already going a lot worse than she might have hoped. Midas had not given her a moment to breathe or prepare; his invasion was already far underway.

Before she could get herself settled at the podium, as an assistant fiddled with the wires attached to her microphone, the audience flooded the air with questions. There was a mix of experienced muckrakers trying to make their comeback and freshmen trying to catch their big break. This was the most heated story of the century, if not eternity. Oedipus was trying her hardest not to screw things up any further; meanwhile, the press did what the press does best.

"So, this army, the Legion of Figments is what they are calling it? Ah, this army, well, what's a Figment exactly?" A dark-skinned Egyptian with thick, black glasses pushed his microphone into the vocal range of the Hegemon. He was quickly bumped aside by a short plump lady with curly brown hair.

"And where did they come from? Nobody has heard of the Figments before now. What are they after? Are they aliens? Did they come to harvest out bodies?"

The Egyptian struggled against his female oppressor and put his mic back in optimal range. "Whatever they are, now that they're kicking our asses, everybody seems to know something. But, everyone's facts are different. Madam Hegemon, what's the official word? Who are the Figments?"

Oedipus understood why the humans called this the press. An unbearable weight was slamming into her chest repeatedly, like a firehose power-washing her will to keep standing. Taking a moment to regain her poise, she tried her best not to let any secrets slip.

"They come from an island..."

With her first query answered, Oedipus had given away a bit too much. The press latched onto that tidbit like remoras on a grazing shark.

"Which island? How many of them are there? Why aren't they more represented in the world government?"

"An island far away, I'm not sure exactly which island off hand." Oedipus was beginning to fall to the endless onslaught of questions. She needed to hold on, just a little bit longer; she could save herself from their suspicions if she could just get some words out beyond this wall of inquisition.

"Madam Hegemon, the island has to be fairly large. It's got to be the size of a small country if all those soldiers were hiding out on it. That limits the options, right? Madam Hegemon, what are your administration's official thoughts on the origin of the invading army?"

The technical assistant gave Oedipus a thumb up. It was time to put on her best Hegemon face. She struck before another member of the press could ask an idiotic follow up question.

"Dear members of the press. I asked you here today so we could have a dialogue about the terrors attacking our lands. I want to impress upon you the importance that you do not fear this army. If you are afraid, the terrors will win. That's what makes them strong, your fear. They will wipe the planet clean, and then destroy it."

The press mumbled for a minute, but they were hardly fazed. A young, white man with a curly, red afro quickly asked a question, filling the silent void with useless noise.

"I've got to ask about the animals. They've got the world's best scientists stumped! I spoke to Doctor Richard Levy, who says he can't even begin to catalogue some of the beasts he's observed. Tell us, Hegemon Epitaph, what are these monsters and where are they from?"

A young Chinese reporter nodded her head in agreement. "There have to be some leads, at least. Which ocean, which region of the globe, at least? Just give us some info and we can probably extrapolate from that and guess which island they're from. Come on, Madam Hegemon, you've got to have something for us. Throw the people of the world a bone, at least."

"No, we don't know which island or sea or ocean they are coming from," Oedipus replied. "All we can say for certain is that their numbers are growing every day. They are learning more about us every day and adapting their strengths to target our weaknesses. I am afraid we will need to take drastic measures to combat them."

"How do you know so much about them? Do you have a mole on the inside? A secret agent planted in their camp?"

"Well, you could say that." Oedipus couldn't reveal that she was, in fact, a Figment. One little slip-up like that could cost her everything. She was the only one with the ability to stop Midas, but she needed her Hegemonial authority to be able to go through with it.

"Who is it? Is it one of their elite? One of the generals? Is he your lover?"

"Is it a human? Did one of the Figments go rogue? Can you trust him?"

"Or is it, by chance, a she? You are a woman, but there aren't too many women in your cabinet. Why is that, do you expect to change it over the remainder of your time in office?"

"Okay, now you're just being ridiculous. " Oedipus said, angrily. "How can you possibly care about such insignificant issues? There is a battle going on for the survival of the planet. You so focused on these tiny problems that you are missing the big picture behind it all. I'm sorry. This press conference is over. I'm going to go try and do something effective against this threat."

Oedipus called an emergency meeting of her cabinet and the world's leaders in the Global Forum, a building constructed in replicate image of the United Nations Headquarters. The late Carrion Son had destroyed the original in a brave but misguided attempt to win Anonymous in one, extremely chaotic act. He might have succeeded had he survived the attack. Of course, international conduct resumed in a secret bunker, but the public demanded their tickets to the circus. The Global Forum had been built to appease this frenzy. From this emergency meeting, the public had been banned, though they massed outside in seething throngs.

Oedipus sat at the front of the large room, staring out at the bevy of people who had been forced to accept her rule. The most trusted members of her cabinet flanked her on either side; them she had hand-picked from the surviving Anonymous players. The governors of each country in the Hegemony sat as her audience, ripe with anticipation for her decision on the current crisis.

Every Anonymous player she contacted had agreed to join her committee and help to rule the world without a struggle. Even a runner-up prize was enough to satisfy these egomaniacal villains. They knew that as long as they sat near enough to the pot of power, some would boil over and reach their bowls.

Oedipus' problem was that the rest of the globe's administration was in the hands of the densest bureaucrats on the planet. Their lack of common sense was so profuse that Oedipus was convinced it must have been a job requirement. A bachelor's degree, five years experience, and an inability to see the truth for what it was.

Their loyalty to her seat was the product of fear, not respect, but she couldn't afford to be choosy with her pieces in this game. She had enough aces up her sleeve that she could probably run with the hand she had been dealt.

Oedipus snickered internally as she took a deep breath. It seemed a funny joke. At first, there had been overwhelming resistance to her ascension to the seat of Hegemon. During her inauguration, less than half of the world's countries sent a representative to greet her. Today, she had attendance from ninety-five percent of the world's representatives. The missing five percent were from countries that had already been slaughtered by Midas' armies. Once everyone was looking for a scapegoat to pin his troubles on, Oedipus finally got the attention she needed to finish her plan.

"As you are all most painfully aware, the Earth is under attack from a dark army, a terrible legion of demons. They are not humans, not beasts, and they are certainly not from Earth. It is difficult to discern whether or not they are even flesh and blood. I can't tell you exactly what they are because even our top scientists have not deduced the answer. What I can tell you is that the soldiers of this army are nearly invulnerable, as our fallen troops in the Mediterranean will surely attest.

"As a race, human beings are perched on the precipice of death. All the creatures that share the earth with us are also in danger. These invaders will not stop until they have snuffed out all life on our planet. They want to turn the entire planet into a chaotic wasteland. Today, we must take drastic measures to ensure we evade extinction." Oedipus' belly spasmed as she spoke plural personal prounouns over and over. She was acting as if she had some deep, biological camaraderie with these idiots; it was a funny feeling, something unfamiliar to the Figment. Her eyes twitched as she tried to keep a straight face.

"And so, I come to my main purpose. I need full approval from my Cabinet and the Forum to unleash an atomic storm. I must ask that we repeal the ban on atomics for the sake of mankind. Additionally, I will ask for all of your atomic reserves to destroy these invaders in one fell swoop."

Silence filled the auditorium. One representative sneezed; it was heard around the world.

After several awkward minutes, Oedipus continued. "Well, doesn't anyone have anything to say? Any questions at all? Can I just go ahead and launch my weapons, already?"

The governor of Japan spoke through his translator. "Honorable Hegemon, I am certain you are aware that as part of the ban on atomics we were required to defuse all the atomic weaponry in our reserves. We do not have any bombs for your requirements."

The Russian governor stood to join his compatriot. "Yes. How dare you ask this of us! We have complied with all the previous Hegemon's whims. We cannot reverse all the grand actions we have taken, just because Solomon's pup orders us to do so."

"Yes, yes, of course, I understand," Oedipus said, "None of you want to throw the first bomb. It's okay. It's crucial that you understand; no state shall be punished for their actions. We are in a time of crisis; a time when some, if not all, deviations from order will be overlooked.

"Do you really think I believe that you destroyed all your weapons? If you do, well, you're bigger fools than I had warranted. I know you've got secret stashes of these things. Just come out and admit it already."

Spain's translator replied in a calm voice. "My liege, with all due respect. As citizens of the world, we all agreed to remove atomic weapons from our arsenals. There are no bombs remaining."

"You've got to be kidding me." Oedipus was working up a tempestuous fury. "The fate of the world is at stake, you imbeciles! Are you so proud that you won't admit to harboring weapons of mass destruction? There will be no repercussions, if you hand them over to me right now. We have got to vote on this immediately, before this building goes down under the hooves of the advancing army."

Andora took its turn at the podium. "Well, couldn't we just bomb the bastards? With planes and non-nuclear ordinance? Our combined forces will be unstoppable!"

North Korea shook his fist in the air. "Hear, hear. We are so powerful, as human beings. With our powers combined, even the walls of Heaven would fall."

Oedipus was getting flushed. "All the soldiers of Turkey, Syria, Iraq, Jerusalem, and all the others that have fallen, they were crushed before the mighty horde. Don't you think they tried to use explosive force? All evidence shows no signs of the army being slowed. In fact, it seems to be growing larger every day.

"It is time we stopped pussy-footing around and took some drastic measures. Our survival is a gamble as it is. If you don't assist me in this effort, your pride won't matter. Nobody will be around to see your embarrassed face."

Oedipus stared out at the slack jawed crowd. Finally, she saw that France was about to stand and announce his own useless idea.

"You know what," Oedipus said, "Don't even start. Okay, fine. Let's try again, another way. If, supposing, there are any usable atomics that someone has accidentally forgotten about, may we use those atomics to annihilate the invading army? Shall we vote?"

A low din filled the auditorium.

Finally, the Governor of the United State. "I don't quite know what's going on, but I've seen some freaky things recently. There's no way I'm going to let those terrors win. I second the motion. Let's vote."

Oedipus let loose a deep sigh she hadn't realized she was holding. "Yes. Fantastic. Please cast your votes immediately; we must take action on this issue as soon as possible."

She watched as the world leaders fumbled with the small electronic voting devices attached to their desks. Like bumbling monkeys, they chose yea or nay with their stubby fingers on its touch-screen.

When all the votes were tallied, the results were projected on the wall behind Oedipus. Yea: 78%. Nay: 20%.

Oedipus clapped her hands. "Thank you all for your support. This is an important step in the survival of our species. Now we must briefly attend to the acquisition of nuclear weapons. Since none of you governors are being particularly forthcoming, I will turn to my cabinet.

"Mr. Minotaur, do you have any nuclear weapons squirreled away?"

The Minotaur nodded. "Yeah. I've got something on the order of one thousand nukes, armed and launchable." The other members of her cabinet mumbled agreement.

"Perfect," Oedipus said, "Thank you all very much for attending this meeting on such short notice. I will personally guarantee that your actions here today will be remembered in the history books as the greatest deed mankind has ever performed."

She knew her words would satisfy the crowd as she prepared to make an exit.

Oedipus stepped off the stage and rushed out to her waiting escape vehicle. She exhaled a deep sigh of relief as she strapped on her safety belt. Such a huge effort she had made today! Deceiving so many people for so long was exhausting, even if they were mostly simpletons.

Her cheeks flushed as she pondered and savored the irony of her situation. It made her feel especially warm and gooey inside.

She really didn't need the atomics to pull off her scheme; they were more useful as a diversion. In a matter of hours, she would be launching more warheads than had ever been simultaneously launched in the history of mankind. The amount of destruction they would wreak was unimaginable by even the most creative auteurs.

It would make a fine diversion from the real dynamite she was planning to ignite, sending spiritual shrapnel right into her Father's heart. If she wanted to remain the unopposed leader of the world after this ordeal, she would need to be able to avoid as many questions as possible.

Precocious

Ophelia was having a wonderful dream. It was a magical vehicle, a Dolorean that could transport her heart to a time more pleasant than the present. Although, any time would fit that criterion.

The Psyche Figment had always admired and respected her next oldest sister, the Figment of Irony. Oedipus had been the only Figment to successfully pass on the voice of Midas by the force of her will alone. As soon as Terra was born, Oedipus had transferred the blessing to her brother; a baptism, she had called it.

As a result, Terra would hear the word of the Master from his birth until the moment it fell from his head to that of the next Scion of Entropy, Ophelia. He had wished and begged with all his heart to stay attached to his Lord and Master, but it was not his fate to keep the blessing.

As far as Ophelia was concerned, he could have kept the damn voice. She was never able to understand exactly what Lord Midas was blathering on about, but his voice was omnipresent in her thoughts. After she reached the age of pubescence, she heard the Master's gospel day in and night out. Most of Ophelia's dreams showed her images of life before this time. This night, she was dreaming of the week before she began her first monthly cycle.

"Young Ophelia, come hither. I have something to show thee." Terra beckoned to his younger sister from a tree he had planted in Castle Figment's garden. He wore a dark black suit, with matching slacks and tie. His hair was slicked back with the oil from a small succulent he was crossbreeding.

A smiling Ophelia skipped over to her brother. "Yes, dearest kin. Is it a present that you have for me? You are such a spoiler!"

Terra laughed heartily. "Ha! Little sister, perhaps I do spoil thee a bit too much. If that is our Master's will, then so it must be. We mustn't complain about it, hmm?"

Terra reached up into the tree and plucked a small sphere from inside its branches. "Look, dearest. This tree, that Lord Midas commanded me to grow, has borne its first fruit. I did not expect it to bloom for another year or two, at least. Because you are my dearest sister, I thought you might help me come up with a name for this delicacy."

Ophelia sucked on her finger excitedly. Ah, the possibilities were endlessly amazing, but she had to pick the perfect name to please her brother. "Um, how about an banalphaquat?"

Terra tossed the shiny cerulean globe up, recatching it at the zenith of his toss. "No, it's too hard to say. Think simpler; think holier."

Ophelia snapped her fingers. "I've got it. Midari. A fruit befitting our Master!"

Her brother nodded with approval. "Yes, I think that will be perfectly appropriate."

He tossed the lone midari to Ophelia. "And now, my sweet, you must tell me how this immaculate fruit tastes."

"Are you sure, brother?"

Terra nodded enthusiastically. "Yes! Absolutely. It is as the Lord wills, because he compels you through me. Get on with it, then. Take a bite!"

Ophelia took a bite, letting the blue juice dribble down her cheeks and spot her dress. "Oh brother, this is truly an ambrosial sacrament. It can only be described as the taste of our Master's will. It is truly...well, I have never dreamed of such satisfaction."

"That's my girl." Terra ruffled Ophelia's hair began to walk away. "Do me a favor and water my garden, dear. I must go commune with Lord Midas."

Ophelia watched him go as she ravenously devoured the remaining bits of sapphire flesh. That was the only fruit the midari tree would bear.

One week later, as Ophelia's first menstruation began, the tree simply snapped in half. Panicking at the sight of her own blood, Ophelia had gone to the garden to search for her brother's advice; she found him weeping by the withered tree.

"Brother, what catastrophe is this? What happened here?"

Terra whipped himself erect and snapped at his sister. ""What do you think happened, dearest sister?" His words were coated with a thick layer of bile. "It seems as though this tree has a much shorter life cycle than expected. When you ate its fruit, you effectively killed it."

"Brother, that's not fair."

He stepped toward Ophelia, stalking her slowly. He began to tear off his clothing, piece by piece. "Fair? No. It's not fair that I spent so long creating and tending this garden, only to have it destroyed by an ignorant whelp. It's not fair that I was unable to taste the pure will of our Lord when it was well within my grasp. It's not fair that an filthy slut like you should be blessed by Midas' sacrament, when you couldn't possibly understand what that means."

Ophelia backed away and began to whimper. "But Terra, is it not Midas' will? Did he not intend for all this to happen?"

Terra slapped his sister, knocking her to the mossy ground.

"Don't patronize me, whore. Can you not hear the Lord already? Do you not detect his presence growing in your mind, germinating from the seeds of the fruit you ate? Even if you do, there's no way you could possibly understand his meaning. You are much too stupid to follow the Lord's footsteps."

He removed his slacks, finally appearing in the fleshy nude.

"Please brother, stop this at once. This is not what Midas would want."

"Oh yes, dear sister. You are certainly the expert on what our Lord and Master desires. For certainly, it is you, not I, who was in direct contact with our Father the longest among our siblings. It is you, not I, who loves the Holy Spirit more than he loves himself. It is you, not I, who should be the sacred Scion of Entropy to greet our Father when he arrives."

Terra pinned Ophelia to the ground with one hand. He slowly clenched his fist, squeezing the air out of his sister's windpipe.

"Damn this place. Damn Lord Midas. Damn everything. I've lost it all to you, you acidic blasphemer."

This was always the point where Ophelia would wake from her dreams, her memory unable to fill in the ending of the story. Her family refused to inform her of the events that occurred later that day; she couldn't imagine how anything could have gotten worse, but she would never be able to know.

The next day, Ophelia woke to the heavy-handed drone of destruction. Buildings were razed as fires blazed. Chaos was consuming all within its grasp.

The Figments were having a grand party, a debutante ball for devoted debauchers. Their bacchanal was carried on the shoulders of one hundred stone soldiers, golems conjured by Midas' manifested will. The stone men wordlessly hauled a large stone platform, fused with their bodies so they could serve no other purpose. The float was outfitted with luxurious sofas for the new lords of Earth to lounge upon. They lazed and they drank; they cheered and they brayed. The Figments relished every minute of watching their new empire burn up in entropic ecstasy.

The invasion of Earth was going perfectly, the human resistance had never stood a chance. Every village their passed was razed away, every city reduced to rubble. Soldiers came and made their stand, only to have their souls released into the ether by their own darkest fears.

Midas commanded a limitless horde of varied demons and ghouls; he was able to shatter the bravest machismo. The nightmare host feasted on human life and order. For every mote of chaos they incurred, their number grew and their power waxed. Like an avalanche of terror or a flock of hungry zombies, their all-consuming momentum would carry them to the ends of Earth and beyond. Nothing could stand before the abominable horde, especially when led by such a vengeful King.

Midas was nearing his full strength. He had grown into a full-size barbarian, while his crystalline antlers had withered away. Nothing remained of his pupal state except two small bumps on his perfectly bald skull. He alone was standing on the Figment Float, shouting orders to his army to maximize the flow of carnage.

Ophelia sat on her own side of the float, watching her family revel in the glory of chaos. Despite her love for her Father and siblings, Ophelia felt desperately out of place.

This destruction, she did not desire.

She heard the psychic fury as pitiful humans were assaulted by their deepest fears. It felt like nails on a chalkboard or an alarm clock on a cloudy morning. Her mouth filled with a taste of metal and her skin began formicating. Something was calling her to wake up, to escape from an unruly enchantment that had been cast upon her.

The joy in this demonic debauchery, it eluded her.

Her siblings made her feel nauseous from head to foot. Lazarus and Valkyrie were kissing and touching each other in the vilest of manners. Their hands ran like spiders, eagerly fondling every crease of each other's bodies. Archimedes and Coelacanth were competing to see who could urinate the furthest off of the float. They continued to drink as they pissed; one hand put liquid in, the other aimed it out.

Lazy Terra was smoking some strange flower that he'd been cultivating for a long time.

"I've been saving this for a special occasion," he said. "Today is a day for celebration."

He sat and blew smoke rings, watching as they floated up to join the complicated labyrinth of charred particles in the sky. So calm and serene, he had turned to other sacraments when the fruit of his Father failed him. The wrath he had unleashed upon Ophelia was nowhere to be found, dissipated like the smoke from his pipe.

Ophelia wondered if she would have felt any better if Oedipus were still alive. Would her sister have viewed all this sin as acceptable? Would she be acting out against her kin if she were still here?

"Ophelia, dear," Midas turned away from his troops to address his daughter. "Why are you so glum? Today is the day for which we have so long awaited. You should be reveling with your siblings."

The sounds of wet kissing blended seamlessly with the sounds of urine soaking the dusty ground.

"I'm sorry, my Lord, "Ophelia said," But this all seems so wrong. This glorified sin and depravity. Does it really signify the Golden Era you are striving toward?"

"I see," Midas began, "So you are judging your siblings' actions? That is not your place. Do you truly think them wrong for celebrating to excess, on this day? The beginning of the end of all days?"

"Master," Ophelia began, "It's not just that. Its, well, I can't help but feel that this celebration is all a bit, well, premature."

Midas laughed aloud. "Hah! Premature. The only thing premature about this situation is your brother Lazarus."

A drunken grunt, followed by heavy breathing was the only response to this uncomfortable barb. Ophelia frowned.

"It was only a joke, my dear," Midas continued. "You've seen the resistance forces crumble beneath our might. Their minds shatter with fear before they can aim their weapons. There is no secret human weapon that could possibly harm us. No mortal could possibly stay the blades of our soldiers."

The orgiastic express came to a jarring halt. Lazarus and Valkyrie fell off their couch with a fleshy thud.

Not one hundred yards in front of the float stood a behemoth of a man, one who could probably shatter the stone vehicle with his massive fists alone. He held a strange creature before him at gunpoint. The beast looked like it had once been a man, but some tragedy had turned him into something more feral. Ophelia the Psyche Figment felt a strange sensation emanating from him. He was a danger, a threat to the plan. The nightmare soldiers could feel it too. They circled around him, keeping separate from him by a careful radius.

"Midas and family. Hello, sah. The Hippo brings a greeting to you and yours. The Epitaph sends her regards. Also, she says, if you don't go back to your home right quickly, you're all going to die."

"The Epitaph?" Midas smacked his lips together, as though the words were covered in peanut butter. "Now why does that name sound so familiar? It's peculiar. That name has a scent to it."

"I'll handle this." Terra stood and stretched his arms. "I can't let a human be stopping us now."

He walked over to Ophelia and handed her a small, blue box. "Look, sis. I'm sorry about how things have been between us. It's important that you follow your heart and support your family, no matter how things look. Especially now, in our time of need. Take care of everyone for me, okay sis?"

Before she could let out a word of protest, Terra had leapt off the float to confront the danger before them.

"A scent of familiarity." Midas continued, ignoring his son's exit.

"Of family."

Quixotic

Petyr watched the drama unfold on the battlefield before him through his rifle's scope. He had sequestered himself on a grassy knoll, so thick with foliage he could lay down and become invisible.

There was some commotion in the arena. Some strange giant had appeared, threatening to shoot the feral man before him if he did not get his way. Petyr couldn't figure out exactly what was happening. Unfortunately, his sniper scope didn't come with hearing aids.

There was only opportunity for one shot. If Petyr missed, Midas would surely send a legion from his horde swooping down on his hiding spot. If he hit the Lord of Chaos, he might be able to escape in the ensuing confusion. Despite death-defying escapes in the past, Petyr didn't want to rely too heavily on his newly discovered ability. Also, Midas' power would probably cancel out his own, leaving him to be the slobbery chew toy for salivating nightmares.

Petyr felt like he had grown an understanding of Orpheus' dilemma. In Greek mythology, Orpheus was a wondrous musician, gifted with talent by the god Apollo. When his wife

Eurydice was slain, he played music so sad it turned the hearts of the gods themselves. The musician traveled to the underworld to retrieve his wife, under strict conditions restricting her return.

In this part of the story, his dead wife trailed behind him as he attempted to escape back to the upper realm of the living. If he were to turn and gaze at her, she would disappear forever. She was silent; Orpheus needed to trust in her ability to follow him out. In the last crucial moment, as Orpheus reached the surface, he turned to glance at his love only to find a pillar of salt in her place.

Petyr feared his relationship with his power might be the same. He had to accept that it worked passively and that it would protect him. If he focused on it too much or tried to abuse it, whatever source was granting him the power might shatter. More simply, he feared that the ability might not work the same as if it was doing its own thing, whatever that thing might be.

Petyr knew with certainty that he couldn't think of the ability as impervious armor, invisibly sheathing him in an immortal cloak. If he jumped in front of a speeding bus, he would most likely still die. If a vat of liquid nitrogen were to freeze him solid, he would still shatter at the slightest touch. There was still too much about the ability that he didn't understand and the present did not seem like a particularly good time to take foolhardy chances. He had wasted most of his luck long ago.

For the first chapter of his life, Petyr had been raised in a small grain farming community in central Russia. It was miles upon miles from the nearest city. Life was simple there. Every season was planned in advance; what to grow, and how much, was determined by an elected committee. During voting season, the most important issues were whether or not the new kindergarten should have a swimming pool or how the dilapidated hospital should be renovated.

Not many people in the commune cared about the shifting world outside their farming bubble. They ignored the reformation of the country's political structure and the emergence of a multiparty system. Nobody cared but Petyr, who would haven given anything to escape from the settlement's temporal black hole. He knew he was changing, and the village couldn't hold him back.

"Ma and Pa," said young Petyr, "I want to go into Moscow. I want to do politics!"

His father spoke in a gruff tone. "No. I refuse. You must stay and help with the harvest."

"But Father, surely you can find someone else to help. I need to do this! I want to learn!"

"I need your fleet feet and swift hands. There is no one else. Besides, you are a child. What role could a child possibly take in the world of politics? Don't make me laugh."

"Mother, please," Petyr begged, "Don't make me stay. You want me to be a successful man, right? I will be the farmer's voice in Moscow. I will make you proud."

Petyr's mother was easily as strong as his father. "No, you will stay and help us with the harvest. It is especially bountiful this year. We will need your muscle and hands. Your father is right. A child like you has no place in politics."

"No," child Petyr yelled, "I will go to Moscow. I will make a difference! You will see!"

Petyr was forced to remain in the village for years after that fight. He couldn't risk running away; the distance to Moscow was too far and the weather too cold. There were not enough cars in and out of the village for him to stow away. The few farmers with vehicles were too close to his family and would not offer him rides.

With no better options for venting his discontent, Petyr began to sabotage the commune's operations.

Rebellious Petyr spent many nights tormenting the dairy farmers at neighboring settlements. He snuck onto their farms late at night and toppled their prize heifers. He was never caught; he never left a trace of his presence.

Eventually, he found himself a partner in crime. Fellow dissatisfied youth Alik Semenov joined him in his late night escapades after a bizarre encounter in the schoolyard. Alik and Petyr attended the only school for all five settlements of the farming commune. Alik was the son of a dairy farmer that Petyr had been attacking regularly.

"Hey," Alik said, "You smell like my farm. Are you the one who's been messing with our cows? Pushing them over in the middle of the night?"

Petyr immediately took the defensive. "So what if I am? What are you going to do about it?"

Alik shrugged. "Nothin'. I just want to help, is all. I think we could pull off some bigger stunts if we were workin' together. I got some ideas that'd be really fun."

Petyr pondered this for a minute. "More people mean more chances to get caught. You sure you're the only one who knows about this?"

Alik nodded.

"All right, let's hear what you've got in mind."

Together, the devious duo continued to wreak havoc on the simple farming commune. Goading each other on, their actions grew more and more bold. A grain silo was mysteriously vandalized with a picture of a cow dancing a jig with the mayor of the commune. One settlement's chickens were set loose in a recently seeded field. Not once were they ever close to being caught. Together, they knew they were invincible.

188

Looking back, Petyr wondered how much of those adventures had been his natural talent, and how much had been the result of his powers. It seemed unlikely that they suddenly turned themselves on. It was more likely that they had been active all his life; he had just been ignorant of their presence. He could have subconsciously forced Alik to join him in friendship; he could have shaped the nights so they would never get caught. All the events he cherished could have been the result of his power and not his natural abilities. The thought made present Petyr nauseous.

During his sixteenth year, a military recruiter from Moscow passed through the village. He was the first in four years. Petyr and Alik begged him to take them to the city so they could wait for their eighteenth birthdays and enlist. The recruiter, surprised to see such enthusiasm in any potential conscripts, agreed. Petyr left without saying a word to his family.

Petyr and Alik lived together in Moscow for the next two years, sharing adventures and drinks and women. When Petyr was jailed for public drunkenness, Alik bailed him out and smacked him sober. When Alik fell ill with scarlet fever, Petyr nursed him back to health. They grew as close as boys could be, without becoming lovers.

Both young men talked their way into good standing with the military such that, when they were both eighteen, exciting positions awaited them both in the service.

Petyr recalled his first mission as an agent of the Russian secret service. He was paired with Alik. Petyr was the agent on point, guns and muscle; Alik was his back up man, an expert of reconnaissance. Their objective was supposedly simple: assassinate the leader of a mid-sized opium cartel.

It should have been such a simple task.

However, the intelligence on the operation was incomplete; the trafficked substances included things much more valuable than opium.

The first part of their mission went smoothly. Petyr and Alik tracked their target's truck to an abandoned factory. He and his henchmen went inside to meet with their business associates. Petyr and Alik attacked by tossing in a flash-bang and running in, guns hot. The drug lord and his acquaintances fell to the partners' furious fire without returning a connecting shot. The young men felt like they wielded guns fired by a higher spirit.

Petyr's second task was to set the scene to look like a gang shoot-out, to deter investigations into government involvement. Meanwhile, Alik checked the truck for the suspected cargo. Instead of opium, he discovered two irate tigers. They leapt for the light as soon as the door opened. Alik was pounced upon and mauled ferociously. Petyr shot at the tigers until they escaped into the darkness outside the factory, but it was too late. Alik's body was cut to ribbons; the tigers' mighty claws had slaughtered him in seconds.

After that mission, Petyr spent all his free time in bars, drinking liquor, or with women, smoking love. Both addictions slowly built a wall around the void where his friend had once lived. He abandoned his duties and fell in with the bad crowd of Anonymous. Petyr only sobered up for the occasional mission, which he completed with ease. He had crafted himself a strict regiment of self-destruction.

Petyr's nerves began to fray. Was the accidental death of his friend and Petyr's subsequent path of self-destruction all part of his destiny altering powers? Was every event in his a decision made by his passive guardian angel, only serving to bring him towards an ultimate destiny?

Damn these abilities! If it weren't for their meddling, Alik might never have died. At least, he could have lived his days out in peace, back on the farm. Petyr wished he could see his parents one last time, to apologize for and explain everything. He'd made so many mistakes, but here was a chance for him to redeem himself. Kill this baddie, save the world. It should be so simple.

Petyr closed his eyes and calmed his jittery heart. He needed all the focus he could muster. It was better to think of this task as though he was just going to tip over the biggest cow he had ever known. Except, instead of a docile dairy cow, he was going after a prize moose with tiny crystal horns, ready to run him through at first sight.

He let the nose of the rifle fall, just a fraction. There was a fine line between tipping cows and tilting windmills. Peter felt ill at ease; Midas could be waiting for him. Did he know that Petyr was a living being, a force that was ready to ram its fist down his throat? Was he walking into a trap?

Midas was distracted in thought, his fingers stroking his chin as he pursed his lips. It was the perfect opportunity to end this foolish game. Petyr prayed to himself that his shot would ring true.

Petyr retightened his grip on the rifle and refocused his target in the sight. Incredible doubt threatened to devour him whole. He couldn't afford to waste this opportunity. Whatever happened, he would trust in his skills as a secret agent and do as he had always done. Superpowers or no, Petyr was going to finish this mission.

"I'm sorry, sah, I can't let ya do that, Epitaph's orders."

Petyr was lifted high off the ground, held aloft by two unforgettable hamfists. He dropped the rifle as the hands squeezed on his neck, exactly as they had done once before. The voice was unmistakable; the gargoyle that had attacked him in the research lab on his final Anonymous mission was haunting him again.

"No," Petyr begged, "No. I. Must." His breath was leaving him.

"Sorry t' do this to ya again, sah. It's okay though. The Hippo and ya, we're like friends, right?"

Not again. Not now.

The Hippo raised Petyr's struggling body up high and threw him like a trebuchet on steroids, away from the climaxing fray.

The wind picked up as a staunch brick wall raced towards Petyr's face.

Redundant

The nightmares encircling the Hippo had no power over him; he didn't scare easily. Their power came from the dark fears and doubts within their prey, and the Hippo was quite unfamiliar with such emotional concepts. The fell beasts knew well enough to keep their distance. The Hippo respected that. The nudist hadn't been so clever. He had tried to hypnotize the Hippo with some strange dancing moves.

The Hippo was far too familiar with the bodily arts to be swayed by some half-bit dancer. He'd made corpses dance with greater feeling than that filthy hippie could ever muster. The naked man's erotic gyrations quickly grated on the Hippo's sense of aesthetics. So, he put a bullet in the nudist's exposed gonads, followed by one to his brain.

That young girl on the float had cried when he did that. Her sadness tugged on his emotions, and made him feel a brief tug of pain. The Hippo understood a hint of what she felt. If anyone had done that to his brother the Hippo, he would have probably cried, too. That is, he might have cried after avenging his brother's death in a whirlwind of fists. Still, he knew he had done no wrong. No, he was only doing his job.

The circle of terrors drew tighter around him. The beasts were still wary, but growing in bravery as they sensed his faltering will. The man on the float, the one the Epitaph had described as Midas, hardly responded to his son's death. He merely stood and stared, stroking his chin as he pondered the situation.

"The Epitaph, you say?" Midas spoke. "Tell me, behemoth. What exactly did the Epitaph send you here to do, hmm?"

"I told ya, sah. Hegemon Epitaph said ya go home or die." He shrugged. "It's up to ya, sah. The Hippo doesn't care either way."

"Ah, I see." Midas began to pace around the float. "And, if we refuse to retreat, how exactly are you going to kill us?"

"Well, sah, the Hippo just proved ya are flesh and blood by shooting that pervert." The young girl was still audibly sobbing. "I guess the Hippo will do the rest of ya the same way. Maybe."

The ring of nightmares constricted a little bit tighter. A particularly bold rat with three heads dashed out and tried to bite the Hippo's foot. He stomped on it with his massive boot; it disintegrated into a puff of dark smoke.

"No, no, no." Midas said. "I think I know this Epitaph; there's no way she would be so stupid. Big man, Mr. Hippo, I could snuff you out like that little rat, any time I pleased. Now tell me, what's the

Epitaph's real plan? What has she got that could possible threaten me?"

There was one thing left on the Hippo's agenda. He fired his pistol a third time.

The Doctor's corpse crumpled to the ground before the Hippo. One bullet to the brain, no chance of failure. It was just like the Epitaph had asked.

This is how our story is going to end? It is far too soon and more than a little bit embarrassing.

It didn't have to end this way. We could have been a contender.

No, sirs. We could have been hiding out on an island in the Pacific right now, concocting artificial life on our own, secluded getaway.

We could be living on the moon, too, but we screwed it up.

No, it wasn't our fault. There was no way around it.

Oh, whose fault was it exactly, getting us mixed up in this Anonymous business?

If it weren't for Anonymous, none of us would exist. Quit complaining and let us pass with some dignity.

Yes. Don't be ridiculous. We never stood a chance. This was our destiny all along.

No, no, no. If we'd been leading us back then, well, this would be a totally different story.

Hush, do we feel that?

We feel something, but what is it? Did someone turn up the heat?

If we're not mistaken, this is the sensation of melting into infinity.

Always waxing poetic, even in the face of doom, we are. How profound.

Don't we know what this is? This is something we have been searching for our whole lives. This is what we strove for, without truly knowing what it was we sought. This is the feeling of freedom.

Yes. This glorious ecstasy is sweeping over our head. It feels like freedom calling us away. No more duty, no more pressing drive to success. It's nice.

Well, gentlemen, it's been a fun experiment. We think it is time for us to head on out.

Oh really, so when the going gets tough, the turds start going, is that it? Oh, we really…Ah. It just hit us. We're sorry about that last comment.

Don't fret a thing, we all made some mistakes, here and there. Are we ready to go?

Well, it's not like we have much of a choice.

Shush, we'll see us on the other side. Goodbye.

The many voices of Dr. Hadjaz could not simply pass on peacefully to the ether. One final stop on their voyage to null space and time called them like moths to a flame, like ships to a siren's lair.

Ophelia's mind was a sink made for siphoning their psychic flow, spinning it away in a tangled skein.

The doctors' ghosts continued to babble on and on, eternally scientists. Like a flock of lost hens, the Doctors Hadjaz squawked and clucked themselves into a whirlpool of consciousness. Ophelia was entirely overwhelmed. She couldn't run, she couldn't scream. Her body was paralyzed by the disembodied persons competing for control over it.

"No!" she screamed. Her ego lashed out like a whip. She forced the devilish motes back to the corners of her mind's cage. This was her body and she wouldn't give it away to anybody.

Even though they were squelched away, the doctors continued to blather in confusion. In less time than it took her to stand, Ophelia had gone more than halfway down the road to the sanitarium.

Somehow, Ophelia knew this was Midas' fault. He wanted to punish her for not being as loyal vessel as her brother had been. Midas' great, zealous son was dead and he was left with an agnostic daughter. In his disappointment, he was punishing Ophelia by filling her thoughts with the drivel of these maddening bees. They buzzed and buzzed, more painful than any number of stings could amount to be.

Ophelia picked up a wine bottle, emptied by one of her alcoholic kinfolk. She smashed it on the stone floor, reveling in the glorious noise of its shattering; the delectable tinkle of bouncing glass gave her a momentary reprieve from the madness inside her.

The respite was brief, a gasp of fresh air to a passenger on a capsized ship. It was too temporary. The voices in her head, she needed to carve them out permanently. She would tear them out of her father's flesh until she heard them no more.

With the jagged half-bottle at the ready, she stalked toward the demagogue who was responsible for all her earthly woes. This was the man who had burdened her with his words for so many years. This was the man who had made her his slave even before he appeared from the sea. He had fooled her family and turned them against her.

Her brother had taught her one thing with his foolish death. The Figments were flesh and blood, just like human beings. There was no difference between them. She could kill this terrible man right now, and end her suffering forever.

Revenge would be so sweet.

"Ophelia, no! Don't," a drunken Coelacanth pleaded, "No, you don't want to do that." He tried to stand, but the liquor had robbed his legs of mobility. The other Figments were too deeply stupefied to comprehend the situation.

Midas turned in time to see Ophelia's mad slash with the broken bottle. He quickly evaded, though the jagged edge cut a swathe through his gaudy robe.

Ophelia lunged again, determined to strike her Father down. Prepared for her attack, Midas swatted her incoming hand. His deft blow forced her to drop the bottleneck; her weapon shattered into hundreds of tiny shards on the stone deck.

Ophelia fell hard on her bottom. A piece of the bottle pierced her skin through her dress, sending chords of pain spiking through her system.

"Ophelia, daughter," Midas began, "Why do you attempt to wound me so? You will only end up hurting yourself. Don't you understand how much I love you? You are so close to me; you are the one who spoke my words so gloriously before my arrival."

Ophelia shook her head, desperately searching for the piece of glass that had cut her rear. The voices inside her head were still squabbling amongst themselves. She needed to get them out; she was only inches away from sheer delirium.

"No, it's not true. You loved Terra the most. Don't deny it; it's true. He embraced you more than any of us could have done. You loved him best for that. Now he's dead and you are taking it out on me."

Midas shook his head. "You are wrong. I love all my children equally. Every one of you epitomizes one of my best qualities. You are the distillations of the most important parts of myself. I am nothing without you. Don't you see?"

Ophelia's cheeks were wet with tears once more. "No, that's not it at all. I get it; I see right through your lies. You're the one who doesn't get it. Me and Terra and Oedipus, we're pointless. We are extra copies of you, Midas. We are your useless clones. My siblings and I, our existences have no purpose other than to poorly reflect one aspect of your own."

Ophelia's fingers started to bleed. She had found the shard of glass, so sharp she hadn't noticed it pierce her skin. "We are the heads to your hydra. If you cut us away, we will surely wither into dust. But you? It doesn't matter a smidge to you. You can just grow whatever kind of head you need in our place. You can grow two instead, if you feel a need for it."

The Psyche Figment stood proudly before her father and drunken siblings. Her hand gripped the fragment of glass tighter. It looked as though her hand was dripping cabernet onto the stone float. "I refuse to be a part of your narcissistic parade any longer, Father."

In one graceful stroke, Ophelia jabbed the fragment of glass into her wrist. She pulled the shard up her arm to the elbow, ensuring a mortal wound. Blood welled immediately from her veins, seeping onto the cloth of her dress.

"Father, you must watch as I perish before your eyes. This is another aspect of yourself that you refuse to admit. You are flesh and bone, just like the rest of us. Your meat is ripe for harvest, just as rare as the flesh of your sons and daughters.

"Contemplate that..." Ophelia's blood loss was draining her consciousness. "Think on it as your fate rushes forward to meet you."

Ophelia stumbled off the float, blood staining her white dress. She fell forward and lay in the dust, looking as though she slept under a blanket of soft pink petals. As her life ebbed, she reached out to grab her brother's dead fingers.

"I forgive you, dear brother. I know you meant well."

Midas picked up the blue box that Terra had left for Ophelia. Neither of them would want it anymore, but merely looking at it disgusted him. He tossed it down onto her fading corpse. The box opened as it landed, spilling its contents onto Ophelia's failing body. Six azure seeds settled themselves into the creases of her dress.

With her last remaining strength, Ophelia took one of the seeds and placed it between her lips, on her tongue. The juice of the seed mixed delicately with the blood from her fingers. She let out a gasp of epiphany.

"I was wrong brother. This fruit, it tastes like...

"It tastes like heaven."

The voices in her head disappeared without a trace, as though they had never been. Ophelia passed, smiling, into infinity.

The Hippo watched tragedy unfold before him, but remained unmoved. His mission was complete; he had no other objectives. Was this the extent of the Epitaph's plan? It hardly seemed effective; the main target was still alive. He wasn't sure what he needed to do next, to escape in one piece.

The Hippo had been given specific orders not to engage Midas directly, but he knew that he wouldn't be able to walk away without a fight.

The nightmare circumference around him had congealed into a seamless wall of darkness. There was no way through it. The Hippo couldn't go around it and couldn't go under it. That left only one route for him to take.

He looked to the sky for inspiration but found a perfect diversion.

Salient

Petyr waited and waited, expecting a bone-jarring crunch to destroy him any second. It never came. Instead, he felt himself suspended in a thin, warm hammock. A tickling sensation spread from the top of his head down his body. When the tickle finally reached his toes, Petyr opened his eyes to find the corporeal world around him had vanished into thin air. Somehow, he had escaped gravity's reins.

The building that had been playing chicken with his face was now somewhere far below him. The giant assassin had fallen to unfathomable depths. Rather, Petyr realized, he had risen like a rocket. He was still shooting upwards, jetting futilely toward the sun.

The rapid ascent affected his mood, and he let out a thrilled whoop against his better judgment. Elevations of this magnitude necessarily associated with rapturous elation. Petyr zoomed through the stratosphere, unencumbered by lethargic gravity.

Casting off the chains of earth below, Petyr felt free for the first time he could remember. He whipped through some cirrus clouds, their wispy bodies trailing behind him like toilet paper stuck to his foot. Petyr dive-bombed a flock of migrating geese, scattering their perfect vee. He laughed aloud and spiraled around a cumulus nebula. There were no rules in the kingdom of the sky.

But a sky was not a sky, without an earth from which it was separated. Petyr's spirits dropped with his gaze, as the world under the sun called him back. There had been a mission, an objective, an obligation. Shackles reattached themselves to Petyr's heart, binding it in place and pulling it tight with chains of spirit.

This journey felt like the dream he had experienced while drinking Brother Bartholomew's tea. Petyr glided lazily and stared down at the battlefield below him. He watched as the Figments quarreled amongst themselves. Drunken rage led to brutal infighting. Petyr saw so many potential futures leap forth from that moment, each tweaked by a minute change in a tiny variable.

A wellspring of time was being tapped for irrigation, but it erupted into a violent fountain from too much pressure at its source. Petyr followed the explosion's flow, rising higher than he had flown before. This level of the sky was supremely serene; matter started to thin into the vacuum of the exosphere. The timespring's spray was spread wide, forming a murky mist.

From each future hidden in the fog of time grew a tiny tendril that reached out to grasp the chains around Petyr's heart. Millions of roaming wisps begged to be set free. Billions of futures longed to become the present.

There were too many possibilities; the number of potential futures was overwhelming. The strands of time bound Petyr once more; he was pulled into the swirling mists and lost his clarity of vision.

Petyr began to fall, spiraling down to the butcher's scene below him. He willed himself to fly again, to halt his descent, but it was futile. The ground was rushing up to meet him; surely, this was the end of his journey.

A black spec on the ground was growing larger eerily fast. Petyr tried to focus his eyes on the blurring shape, but was unable.

As it grew nearer, the black blur took on the form of a great black serpent lunging from the ground with a gaping maw, hoping to catch Petyr and swallow him whole. Winged legions of chaos were rushing up to attack their Master's foe. The earthbound army of chaos had merged into a terrible colossus to destroy him in his helpless descent. Petyr was falling at terminal velocity towards a painful demise, fodder for nightmares eternally ravenous.

It was unimaginable. If, years ago, he hadn't traveled to Moscow with Alik, this wouldn't be an issue. He could have opted to pursue a peaceful life on the farm with his family. He could have raised a child with a cute girl from across the wastelands. He could have grown old in peace, possibly buried in happiness.

The current situation was unacceptable.

Petyr crossed his arms across his chest, then spread them wide like a human airplane. His rapid movement sent a ripple of concentrated emotion screeching down toward the rising chaos serpent. Slits of bright earth appeared along the blackness of the draconian demon. Its body was fracturing, eroding from the force of Petyr's will.

Petyr fell faster, eager to return to the ground and finish his mission. There was time enough to reclaim his perfect life after this ordeal was through.

The serpentine nightmare's jaws snapped shut just behind his rigid feet, but the vacuum of his wake tore the dragon's head to pieces. The rest of its body crumbled as Petyr zipped past it. The great beast disintegrated into black dust, swept away into burgeoning wind.

The ground rushed up, faster and faster. Petyr kept his eyes open; he wasn't going to just turn his vision away from his destiny any more. If this were the end of his tale, he would greet it with a jovial grin.

Instead of crashing into the ground, Petyr touched down as gently as a goose might groom its goslings. His feet met the ground with a padded sigh. A powerful wave of air expanded from Petyr's position, kicking up dust in a rapidly growing ring.

All eyes were on him, but not a mote of sound traveled through the air. The drunken Figments, the giant assassin, and Midas all silently observed their extraterrestrial visitor.

Midas clapped softy, cutting a swathe through the heavy silence. "Very cool. Awesome, in fact. That was a very nice entrance. I take it that you, whoever you are, are the one who has been causing me so many problems?"

Petyr replied as coolly as possible. "I don't know what you're talking about." He was still focused on regaining his legs' mobility. The incredible stunt landing had seemingly robbed them of their normal function: locomotion.

"Oh, come on. You must have felt it, too. When I arrived at this plane, I was unable to reach my full potential. My growth was stunted, delaying this glorious day. Some entity was trying to stymie me. I hope that I caused you a little grief, too. And now look at this. You conveniently show up to try and stop me as my invasion is at the threshold of success? How ironic and unfortunate for you."

"Yes," Petyr replied, "I'm here to stop your wanton destruction. You're damn right this is a glorious day. You're going to remember it for a very long time. Rather, I'll be the one who will remember. You won't have that ability for much longer."

Petyr's legs felt like they were attached to long slabs of wood, unable even to bend.

"Needless destruction? Idiot human, you know nothing of which you speak." Midas spat on the dust at his feet and ground it into mud. "I don't know what your game is, silly mortal, but it ends here with me."

As he spoke his last words, Midas broke into a trot. He charged at Petyr, still stricken with immobility.

The distance closed quickly as Midas quickly accelerated to his maximum speed. He lowered his head, revealing that his two short horns had begun to radiate like a glowing smile. Midas' skull careened toward Petyr's chest; Petyr prepared himself for the pain of his innards being crushed to threads.

At the last second, Petyr remembered how to move. This was all too easy, just like tipping a heifer. He twisted his balance, flowing with the charge. Contrary to popular perception, the biggest bovines were easiest to topple.

Using muscle memory alone, Petyr was able to turn Midas' dash attack on its head. Thanks to a simple trick of bodily physics, the spy had a demigod trapped under one knee. Midas was left face down in the dusty earth, his arms imprisoned under his own weight. Petyr pulled out his pistol and placed it at the back of Midas' head.

"Ok, now you're going to explain some things to me before I blow your head off."

"Get your hands off of me, you filthy pauper!" Midas struggled in vain to escape Petyr's pin. "What have you done to me, did you sap me of my power? Who do you think you are?"

"No, no, that's enough of that," Petyr said, removing the safety from his gun. "I will be asking the questions today. It's my turn to get some answers."

Trapped, Midas lashed out with his tongue. "Who are you compared to me? I am a deity, a true force of nature."

"You are only what your disciples make you to be. You have no true power on your own. Your will is brittle and weak. You waste it on the creation of those asinine terrors. You pit all your efforts into this destruction, for what purpose? Is there no more noble cause to divert your hand?"

Midas closed his eyes, his forehead creased. "I know those words, but I have not heard them spoken for eons. It's been an eternity.

"Petyr, is that really you? Oh, it is. I should have known. This place has got your scent sprayed all over it."

Petyr was jarred, but he held his position. Whatever Midas was thinking, it was most likely a trap to weaken his resolve. One second of weakness could give the demigod more than enough opportunity to escape.

"I don't know who you are talking about, but it isn't me." Petyr pressed the barrel of his gun hard into the back of Midas' neck. "Tell me why you are so hell-bent on destroying this planet. Why do you want to take such a beautiful reality and erode it into non-existence? What's your purpose? Are you such a narcissist that you think your vision for the future is the only one that matters?"

"Oh, you haven't changed a bit, Petyr. You still don't get it, do you? I'm not doing this for myself. The razing of this world has been a long time coming. There is too much order; the balance of the universe is skewed. My presence is just a corrective measure, the natural way of things. I guess you were never very good at going with the flow. You always had to speak your mind, always had to take a contrary position.

"Well, this is one battle that you shouldn't waste your time fighting. You can't take on the universe itself, Pete. It's much, much bigger than you."

"I beg to differ," Petyr said. "I defeated most of your army in a single blow. I've got you at an endgame. I'm not sure how I'm doing it, but I am going to stop this pointless destruction. For some reason, I've grown attached to this ugly world; I don't think I like the thought of a bastard like you ruining it."

"Ho, you are such a fool," Midas laughed. "Petyr, Petyr, ever the sentimentalist. Well, you may have been able to dissolve most of my troops, but there was one soldier that you never stood a chance against. Can you feel it now as it pokes around your core, tearing you to bits? That's my prized creation, the ultimate manifestation of my entropic dreamscape.

"If you can't stop it, well, the universe's fate is far out of your hands."

A wriggling sensation grew in Petyr's intestines. Something was alive inside him.

"What is this?" he screamed. "What did you put inside me? Tell me, you bastard, or I'll blow your head off!"

Midas chuckled softly. "Oh, boy. I didn't put anything inside you. It found its way inside you on its own. Or rather, you laid a path to let it slip right through your defenses. You see, Petyr, though you claim to be fighting for the sake of Order, you are doing it in a very chaotic manner.

"This devil, my precious, it's feeding on the entropy within you. The turbulence in your will is so great that my pet was drawn to you like a bloodhound to a rabbit."

"Call it off! Call it away, right now. I'm not kidding around." Petyr cocked the trigger on his pistol; the time for games had long passed.

Midas shook his head. "I'm sorry, there's nothing I can do about that. It's out of my hands. I am just as vulnerable to the beast as you are, except I know how to cut off its route inside me. Maybe you should have solidified your self before you attempted to come organize the disciples of chaos."

Midas jabbed Petyr with an elbow that he had managed to free from underneath himself. As Petyr fell off balance, Midas rolled away in an attempt to escape.

Petyr could feel his insides rearranging themselves, his tissues being rent asunder. There was no time to think, to process the situation. As his muscles were torn to shreds, the gun in his hand managed to fire four times. Each shot was perfectly aimed; there was no possible escape for Midas.

Through excruciating pain, Petyr felt something unraveling. At first, he thought it was his body being unspooled by the mysterious terror. But a strange intuition told him the feeling came from outside him.

The bullets slowed as they approached the Lord of Chaos, but his reactions were equally geared down. Another strange wind picked itself up as time decelerated to a molasses crawl. Closer and closer, the bullets inched their way forward, strung along invisible threads of destiny. Midas awaited his defeat with a mask of regret stapled to his face.

The first bombs fell; they rained a torrent of destruction to flood the battlefield and cleanse its dirty heart.

Triage

"Oh, yes! God, yes!"

Oedipus detached her sweaty body from her lover's. Their skin stuck together as she peeled herself away, breathing heavily. She rolled on her back and looked up at the ceiling silently, staring at the stars spiraling through her vision.

Oedipus sighed. "If ever I ask you to remind me why I love you, let's just do that again. Okay?"

Petyr laughed and rolled over on top of his wife. The couple giggled into each other's lips as they kissed.

"That sounds like a very good plan," Petyr whispered into Oedipus' ear. "But I'm going to put my pants back on for now."

Oedipus put on a playful pout. "You're such a party pooper. Always ready to get working and run away from me."

Petyr rolled his eyes. "I'd better get into the office, honey. You know how my patients get when I deprive them of even a few minutes with me. They'll be calling for malpractice in no time."

Oedipus purred at her husband. "But you know how I get when I'm deprived of you, too. I'll be calling for something a whole lot more exciting than malpractice, if you know what I mean."

Petyr pulled on some pants and a long sleeved shirt from the closet. He tied a black and white striped tie around his neck. "I will be back before you even notice that I'm gone."

Oedipus grabbed Petyr by the collar and pulled him close.

"Yeah, right. You go make your money. I'm making you something special for dinner tonight, darling. I won't tell you what it is, but know that it's going to be something extra spicy. Think about that while you're at busy twiddling your thumbs at work, my dear."

Petyr blushed. "My goodness, you make it hard for a guy to leave the house!"

Oedipus winked and kissed her man goodbye. "That's what she said."

Petyr managed to drive to his office, adjourn a staff meeting, and start reading his patient's charts before the earthquake shook half of New Minx city to the ground.

His practice was located on the outskirts of the city, but the population in that area was dense.

Immediately after the quake, patients flooded his office, quickly filling up every examination room. Those rooms with better equipment were reserved for the more urgent patients, with open wounds. As the morning stretched on, more and more patients came to seek aid, forming a line around the block.

EMTs were deployed from neighboring cities to help with the disaster. The nearby cities had suffered some damage, but none so severe as the collapse of New Minx. Freeways crumbled, crushing hundreds of vehicles and their passengers. The tallest building in the city broke in half, surrendering the title it had claimed for the last two decades. This was the worst crisis the city had seen in years, the first magnitude eight earthquake in over a century.

Petyr's waiting room was turned into a makeshift sick bay. Injured citizens were forced to wait there for admittance, grumpily slumped in chairs or against a wall. If the injury were simple enough, the patient would be treated on the spot, without entry to the exam room.

One patient arrived in an angry huff. He claimed to have a previously scheduled appointment for the day. He forced his way through the crowd milling about outside the clinic. He stepped through and stumbled over the injured people packing the waiting room until he reached the front desk.

"Excuse me, miss," he said to the receptionist. "My name is Midas Budgerigar. I had an appointment today at ten o'clock. It is now half-past eleven and I have not even been called into the waiting room. I demand to see my doctor immediately!"

The receptionist glanced at the psychotic stranger before her and the ailing people around him. "Are you serious? Did you look around before you opened your mouth? No, don't answer that question."

"So, you're saying these hypochondriacs are more important than some who is genuinely sick? I need a refill on my medicine, and I won't leave until I get that prescription."

A burly patient in the waiting room waddled over to the conversation; a falling gargoyle had crushed his foot.

"Now wait one second. Who are you to say that you're more important than the rest of us? I nearly had my skull cracked open by a falling piece of art today; I think my broken foot requires more urgent attention than your pill popping fix, Narcissus."

Mr. Budgeriar scowled at this offender. "You dirty sociopath, you don't know anything about my situation. If I don't get my pills, I could go into withdrawal and die. Do you know what that's like? It's a slow, painful death filled with hallucination and vomit. At least a blow to your dome puts the lights out quickly. No chance to suffer."

"You sick bastard. I hope your family fell into some crack and died. Miss Receptionist, I want to talk to the Doctor and get this pervert out of here. He's just a junkie preventing all these upstanding citizens from getting proper treatment."

The receptionist sighed. Another day, still no respect. "All right, I'll call the doctor out from the back. It's not like he's probably doing something important like suturing up someone's open wound or anything like that. No he's probably just sitting on his butt, watching everybody suffer."

The receptionist dialed up the doctor's priority line. "Doctor Dmitriev, patients are asking to see you and won't shut up about it."

Petyr, who had already been drawn to the front of his office by the commotion, stepped into the waiting area.

"Stop this at once, or I will send you all to a different facility. Both of you make me sick, trying to decide which lives have more value than others. That is not your job. We are working as hard as we can to fix the patients already roomed so we can move on to less urgent cases.

"It is not up to you to decided who gets to come back. I'm the one with the experience to know what it dangerous; it's my office. I'm the one who has taken the Hippocratic Oath. The responsibility for prioritizing care falls to me. If you don't like it, I suggest you seek care elsewhere. I am sworn to do no harm, but I have no obligation to serve your whims."

The complaining patients shut up, but their faces were lined with discontent.

Petyr turned to the receptionist. "I need to go make a phone call. If these morons give you any more trouble, I give you permission to call in the military."

Petyr stepped outside and squinted in the bright sunlight; squinting at stitches under fluorescent lights did a number on his eyes.

He tried phoning his apartment, but Oedipus didn't pick up. She always picked up within two rings, if she heard the phone. She was especially quick, that way, always waiting to hear from her love. No, he assured himself, she had to be fine. It was something in the phone lines; that was all.

"Dr. Dmitriev!" A young EMT hurriedly hailed Petyr out of his destructive introspection. He jogged over to Petyr's position as his partners began to remove patients from the back of the ambulance. Something was familiar about this EMT, but Petyr couldn't quite place his face. It was as if though his features slowly shifted over time.

"We have two more patients in the back right now. One is a sixty-two year old female. She has no visible external injuries, but she was found underneath a fallen telephone pole. Her responses are sluggish, she may have serious head trauma.

"The other is a sixteen year old male. Some falling glass cut open the posterior tibial artery. He may bleed out. They need treatment immediately, but our vehicle is running out of supplies. Can we treat them here?"

Petyr detachedly shook his head. "All of the beds in this facility are filled with wounded victims. What should we do with them? I don't know, there's not enough space to give them the care they need."

The EMT was adamant. "Here they come, just take a quick look at them and see if there's something you can do. Their situations are pretty dire. Maybe you have some patients that are in stable conditions. Maybe we can give these patients their rooms."

The other EMTs rolled over a pair of stretchers with patients strapped in on top. Petyr looked at the pair of victims and nearly fainted from stress.

The sixty-two year old woman was his mother.

"Oh, Petyr, don't be silly. I know it's Oedipus and your first anniversary. I just want to drop a little something off."

"No, mom, that's quite all right. You don't have to do anything for us. We've got some special plans. At least, I think we do."

"Petyr, you are such a boy when it comes to things like this. I really like this one, so I don't want you screwing things up. I will come into town with a little surprise for you to give her."

"Mom, if the people at work catch you doing that, they'll laugh at me."

"And they should! If you can get a girl, you should know how to keep a girl. Now, I won't take no for an answer. I'll be coming in the morning, you can take me out to lunch to show your gratitude."

"Mother..."

She had come in to the office for lunch, just as planned. However, she would be eating from a tube, if at all.

The other stretcher held someone just as familiar. The bloody boy was Alik, son of Petyr's neighbor and a frequent friend.

"Hey, Doc."

"Hi Alik, what's happenin', dawg?"

"Oh, man. Dr. D, you really need to catch up on your slang. Tell you what. I can help you with that, if you can help me with something."

"Shoot, son."

"I need to shadow someone for a day of work for my Careers and Futures class. Can I come watch you in the office?"

"Yeah, sure. Come in anytime after ten, tomorrow morning. I'll be free to show you a couple things. You can see how cool it is to be a doctor these days."

"Erm, yeah, right. Sure, that's fine. I'll see you around noon then. Tomorrow."

True to his word, he arrived at close to noon.

The lives of two people close to Petyr's heart were thrust into his hands. Their lives had been taken in by his gravitational pull, and had suffered for it. If they had stayed at home, they might have avoided injury. Now, both patients were on the brink of death and it was his responsibility to figure out how to save them.

What was the cost to save one of the two? Another gravely injured patient, expelled from his sickbed? Could he spare the time to save both of them, or would he have to choose between them?

"Can you transfer them to Sister of Mercy? They've got to be more prepared for this crisis than we are."

"Doc, Mercy is down. The whole north wing collapsed. As far as they can tell, they lost all the wing's patients; the wing's supplies are gone, too. They are hurting for room, just like you.

"Besides, roads are completely congested with wreckage. These two wouldn't make it very far, certainly not all the way down to the center of the city. They must be treated here if they are going to get treated at all."

Petyr shook his head. "I don't know, I don't know. I'm not the one who should be making this decision."

"Doctor, keep it together. We need an assessment right away," the EMT said. "Can we treat them here? Otherwise, we're going to lose them both. You are the person with the authority to make this choice. It's in your hands."

"I'm sorry, give me a minute. Let me make a quick phone call."

Oedipus would know what to do. She always knew the right decision. Petyr flipped open his cell phone and rang up his apartment. Still no answer, something was wrong. The EMT stood watching with his arms crossed, his foot tapping a listless rhythm.

This was not what Petyr was hoping to find in his life.

A dry wind began to blow through the parking lot, carrying a season's worth of dead leaves in its flow.

Urchin

Petyr the urchin was having the best day of his young echinoidian life. The algae in his sector of the tidal basin were particularly delicious. Something about the sunlight in this region must have made their chlorophyll particularly excitable. Maybe the depth of the water distilled sunbeams down to only the optimal wavelength of light for their usage. Maybe it was something to do with the consistency of the sandy bottom. Petyr was much less concerned with the why and how compared with the fact that it was purely delicious. The algae's aura was closer to that of kelp, a rare delicacy that Petyr had only tasted once, by luxurious accident.

He lazily grazed, savoring the simple pleasure of eating well. There was no pressure today, aside from the water on his spines. He felt no drive to reproduce or to defend himself or to do anything except focus on his pleasure. It was a truly perfect day for a young urchin under the sea.

Petyr was young, but he was not naive enough to think this situation would last. His brother urchins would soon discover this sacred grotto and come to claim it as their own. Subtle currents would carry morsels of macroalgae to the waiting mouths of nearby urchins. They would slowly clamber down from their rocky perches to the sandy sea floor, microtubules pumping heavily. They would gobble up as much food as possible, until a conflict of interest caused one of them to bump into another urchin.

Petyr's primary defense, a carapace of spiny appendages, would do little good in a fight with other urchins. The other urchins would be immune to his venom and his pushes. However, his opponents were similarly equipped and would be equally unable to do much to him; any battle would end in a stalemate. Eventually, however, the sector would be flooded by gluttonous urchins eager to siphon away all the delicious nutrition.

The urchins were a nearly unstoppable, ecosystem-ravaging force. Once a region's resources were leeched away entirely, the slothful creatures would migrate away, back to their solitary existences. They would transform their feeding ground into an urchin barren, devoid of life, horribly infertile.

Somehow, the simple creatures could continue on without regret. The urchins had small brains; cause and effect were of little consequence in their daily life. They would search every square foot of ocean until they found another treasure trove of sustenance. Soon enough, that too would be overrun by the underwater hedgehogs and picked clean.

Petyr knew that this was his grand opportunity, a chance to gorge himself without bumping into any other urchins. He ate as fast as he could, his ventral mouth scooping and scraping up every morsel in reach. It took all his focus not to reingest the excrement flowing out of his anus past his mouth. Petyr was so lost in his tiny mind that he failed to notice the great shadow growing rapidly larger on the sea floor.

He was snatched up off the ground and rocketed up toward the water's surface. Gigantic furry paws held him firmly against a forested chest. Petyr had been scooped up by an urchin's worst nightmare, a sea otter.

It was only a matter of time now; his fate was already sealed.

The otter broke through the surface and assumed a reclining position, resting on his back in the salty water. Hedonist of the sea, he carried Petyr on his buoyant belly. Petyr felt as though a jungle of fur had sprung up around him. It dulled his senses and self-awareness. He panicked and tried to run away but was unable. The furry belly of an otter was nothing like the ocean floor. He was trapped like a fish out of water.

However, not all was a loss for the poor urchin.

Petyr felt the direct sunlight for the first time in his existence. The ultraviolet rays warmed his spine and he felt the true meaning of love. He became aware that this great icon in the sky was the truth behind the flavor of the algae. His radial symmetry had met its match. Though he could not see it, Petyr felt the sun's globular grace bless him all over. The great burning sphere in the sky was infinitely symmetric, pure radiance.

He stretched his spines skyward, grasping for a better sense of heaven.

Another shadow fell across his body. A rock slammed down onto his hard shell and retreated, blocking the light of the sun. Heaven suddenly felt further away than ever.

The rock fell again, a pendulous hammer striking with ferocious rhythm. It beat savagely, competing with the murmur of Petyr's simple heart.

A hairline fracture split through Petyr's shell, reducing his symmetry to tri-fold. The three shards of his shell clung to his sticky meat. An antagonizing pain ripped through his flesh, so intense that it bordered on ecstasy. The three shards of his shell clung to the sticky, fleshy body underneath; his core was the only thing holding him together.

Another stone blow split the crack open wider, exposing Petyr's juicy core. The furry floater squealed with glee. Victory and dinner were within its reach. It stuck its tiny thumbs in the cracked shell and pulled it apart. The salty sea air cut into

Petyr's flesh like an icy dagger. He quivered with joy; the pain sent him into an orgasmic euphoria.

The sea otter placed its lips on the biggest cracks and tongued Petyr's flesh. It tickled him and frightened him, but he was unaware of anything but his joyous connection to a god he had just met a few minutes ago. This life had been worth living, if only for the precious few minutes with golden perfection. Before he passed into the murky unknown, he was given a dose truth. It calmed his heart while his body was slowly tasted.

As his flesh was sucked from its protective armor, Petyr's mind began to dim. His memories flickered away as his body was chewed beyond recognition. The fair god of the skies faded away as an eager esophagus pushed Petyr's meat into a starving belly.

A deep, penetrating darkness fell over Petyr's mind.

This was not the way his story was meant to end, let alone how it began.

A moist wind began to blow.

Voracious

Petyr woke to a vision of nothing and everything.

He found himself in a purely white room. He assumed it was a spherical chamber of some sort; lines indicating the positions of walls and corners were nowhere to be found.

The area was completely devoid of matter, but it was full of an invisible presence. This plane was made of pure substance with no hint of style.

Petyr glanced down at his body, but found he wasn't there. Something or someone had rendered him incorporeal.

Though he had no stomach, Petyr was aware of a terrible hunger. Though he had no mouth, he knew that he needed to consume sustenance to survive.

So, he instinctively began to devour the substance around him. Starting at the exact center of his consciousness, Petyr expanded ever outward. There was no end in sight to the realm of substance.

Once, Petyr looked inside himself to check the substance he had guzzled. It looked the same, but was no longer pure substance. It belonged to him now; it had his scent about it.

Petyr ate and ate for what seemed like an eternity. He felt himself grow bigger as he consumed more, though he was unable to tell relative sizes in the unbordered whiteness. After what could have been minutes or millennia, Petyr realized he had gobbled up everything within reach.

Looking around, Petyr saw an empty blackness, flawless as the white that had surrounded him on his arrival. The black void was different from the white, empty and cold; there was no substance there, nothing at all.

As suddenly as his hunger had arrived, it disappeared. Petyr felt stuffed. He had somehow absorbed far more than his limit. He was compelled to evacuate everything that he had swallowed. He shrank back down to nothingness, a keen sense of relief washing through his mind. The substance surrounded him once more, tempting his appetite.

He consumed it again until he was sated; he vomited it away when he thought he might burst.

Soon enough this pattern became as simple as breathing. Petyr filled himself with substance, and released it when he could no longer hold it inside his sphere of influence.

After a million or so repetitions, Petyr grew bored. His was a solitary existence; the tedium of repetitive forced failure eroded the sheen from substance. He wished there were some other spirits like him that he could talk with about his piercing loneliness.

Why do I exist? I am the only creature alone in the darkness. Am I compelled to complete this inane cycle of ingestion and vomiting over and over until the end of existence itself? Why must I suffer so?

After a particularly lonesome cycle, Petyr decided to try his next expansion a little bit differently. As he ballooned out to his maximum girth, he imagined shapes and colors into the substance inside him. An intricate mandala spun around inside his boundaries.

The substance took the form of his will easily, it seemed like it had been made for that purpose all along. Petyr grew quite fond of his artwork; it filled some of the lonely void at the core of his being. He stayed engorged as long as his will would let him, trying to savor the beauty he had manifested. However, every time he shrank back to his minimal size, the substance that escaped his sphere reverted back to an unadulterated state.

Petyr quickly mastered the technique for creating colors and shapes, quickly moving on to more intricate sculpting. He was able to imagine three-dimensional spaces, creating a vast universe full of perfect globes and shining stars. He manifested a grand stream of clockwork energy to animate one of his sculptures. It could be perfectly symmetric one second and grossly asymmetric the next.

A masterwork of complex imaginary design, Petyr next created a universe that was both symmetric and asymmetric at the same time. When this perfect creation was reverted to substance, Petyr lost all hope. He wished his existence could end, but his hunger was already compelling him to start reabsorbing the substance.

One last time, Petyr was determined to try his hand at creating perfection. He would create something so great that the darkness outside would be unable to resist its existence. No force in the universe would make him lose this creation, not this time. If he felt compelled to to wither away, he would overextend himself instead. He would force his will into the empty void and would lead his fate through an unknown universe.

Petyr willed an intricate space, weaved from an ethereal skein. Every planet, every star, and every atom was connected in a complex dance. This was a song for the heavens, one that Petyr wished someone else could hear. But there was not a soul in the surrounding universe.

And so, Petyr decided to create himself an audience. He stirred up some muck on a blue-green planet and animated it by linking it to some spare time. The first cell was born; it was a clockwork marvel.

Petyr watched it grow and divide and die, but he was not dissuaded. He tried creating it again and again, until he had designed a viable system for life.

He tinkered with the cells, making them more varied and powerful. He gave everything unique abilities and traits; he gave them all secret names. Evolution exploded from his fingertips; he transmogrified every bit of life he touched.

As life grew more complex, individual creatures found themselves tangled up in each other's lives. Their interactions developed into a tiny meta-dance within the greater ballet. They began to improvise this dance, choreographing steps all on their own. Their decisions surprised their creator, who could only sit and watch.

Eventually, the tiny beasts developed self-awareness. Only then did they understand true loneliness. When he saw the first human beings question their existence, Petyr shed an invisible tear of joy. The tiny folk were busy talking about him, giving him a name.

They saw his face in their cars, the stars, and electric sockets; they saw his face as one of their own. The humans praised his work and sang him songs of their own creation. They were approaching their fullest potential; Petyr had filled them with as many aspects of himself that he understood. He was overjoyed; this last attempt at substance manipulation had been successful beyond his wildest dreams.

And so, Petyr fell in love with his creation; overwhelming emotions voided his memory of the loneliness he had felt for so long. He built himself an avatar and lost himself within the world of his creation

Petyr was so distracted by the swelling chorus in his stomach, he failed to notice the shifting darkness around his substance. Hundreds of glowing white spheres of substance had appeared, drawn to the cosmic song, compelled to lend their ears.

They crowded closer and grew in number until there was no room any more. Instead, the spheres began to absorb one another in furious cannibalism.

Petyr's sphere remained untouched, content to continue singing its song as the spacious void surrounding it grew smaller and smaller.

This was not the life he was looking for, but it was the purest truth he had found.

Cutting through the warmth of embryonic darkness, a cold wind blew.

<u>Wake</u>

Petyr woke to find himself in a world of endless darkness. As his eyes adjusted, the black veil slipped away and muddled shapes began to appear. Tall, arched ceilings littered with religious icons indicated he was in some sort of cathedral. He was sitting on a hard, stone pew at the center of the holy building, surrounded by hundreds of black-garbed figures.

The dark strangers were in various stages of exaltation. Some were bowing toward the front of the cathedral; others sat with their arms extended to the heavens. A group near the altar writhed in place with arms wrapped tightly around their shoulders. They sang a wordless melody, accompanied by an obscured organ. Wild black dancers whirled like dervishes among the audience.

A white casket adorned with blue and purple roses lay near the altar, indicating the celebration was not entirely joyous.

Petyr's neighbor seemed different than the others members of the congregation. He appeared to be less invested in the ritualistic ceremony. Instead, he was muttering curses under his breath.

"So, who's funeral?" Petyr whispered.

The old man turned to gaze at Petyr with empty eyes. "Why, it's yours, of course."

"Excuse me?"

"It's mine, too. Everyone here is approaching expiration, although it is well past due for most of us. But in the end, it's your funeral."

"But, I'm alive. I'm sitting right here, next to you. My body definitely isn't up in that casket. This can't be my funeral."

"No, I think you're dead, boy. Dying at the very least. These visions you're having, well, they're your spirit trying to stave off what your body knows to be true. It's trying desperately to wake you out of your stupor, so that you might try and save yourself. You're finished, unless you can do something to fix what ails you."

"And how exactly am I supposed to do that, may I ask? I'm not even sure what's wrong with me. And-wait a second, how do you know what's happening to me?"

"Are you dense or just under-ectoplasmic? Sorry, lad. Etherial humor. You lose touch with what's funny when you've been dead long enough."

"Thanks for that," Petyr said, "I suppose. But I still don't get it. What's happening to me?"

The old man shook his fist. "Seriously, though. Have you been paying any attention to your visions? You lived the life of a man whose will superseded all others. You know the burden that comes with the power of decision. You've lived the life of a creature with hardly any will at all; you should know the helplessness that entails. You saw a glimpse of your true life and the power your real form can wield.

"You've got the potential of a omnipotent entity, but you can't even use your mortal powers of deduction. You've gone soft, boy. I see now why you're on the edge of death. Just use your abilities to save yourself. It's simple."

Petyr scoffed. "Just rewrite the world? Pick the present from a different timeline? Even if I understood how to do that, I don't know if I could allow myself to do it. I mean, where does it end? I must have some guidelines. Some rules. Right?

"Say, if at a certain juncture, I choose a timeline where I avoid getting shot, that borders on making sense. I can chalk that up to luck and probability. But there are an infinite number of futures that can branch from any given moment.

"I can will the shooter to miss me or I can allow myself to get wounded. I could let myself be shot but have the bullet bounce off my chest and ricochet until it kills the shooter. It's unlikely, but it's possible. If I wanted to flex my mental muscles, could suddenly reverse the law of gravity and send the bullet and every other bit of matter into a vacuous void. Stranger still, I could transform everyone into a cockroach, except myself, and stomp out all the life on earth in a destructive dance. Or, if I wanted, the world could become a blue, two-dimensional matrix, right? That's within my power?

"I don't want that kind of responsibility. I can't subject the entire universe to the whims of my subconscious. It's too much power for one person to have."

"That's exactly why you're the right entity for the job. You respect the weight that your decisions hold." The old man smiled. "To be frank, you're the only entity for the job. The job only exists because you exist, so that point is moot."

"But if I'm the only person with free will, then everyone else must fall to my bidding. I'm the only person in the world whose opinions truly matter. I'm the center of the universe because I'm the only being with meaning? I don't want to live in a world like that. It's so empty and sad. I mean, what's the point? Is there a purpose in any of this?"

"The urchin enjoyed his brief existence, though he did not have any true purpose. He had no say in the way things played out. There is as much purpose in it as you deem there to be purpose, Petyr. The world is a reflection of your wills and desires, after all."

Petyr squinted at the old man. Though he looked familiar, his features were just out of focus such that Petyr couldn't recognize him. Flickers of familiar faces flashed through the man's features, never quite settling on anyone in particular.

"Have we met somewhere? How do you know who I am?"

The man's features congealed for half a second. Petyr was staring himself in the face. Before he could speak, the mask redissolved into an indefinite mass.

"Petyr, I am me, I am you, and I am everyone we know. But yes, we have met before. You might know me as Bob."

"Excuse me? As in Bob, the deity the Order of Builders worships?"

"That's only one facet of the prism. In reality, they were worshipping you. They were just going at it in a roundabout way, through the act of praying to me."

"I don't follow you. It sounds like they were praying to you, not to me."

"Only vectorally! Oh, Petyr, if only you were better at math, this would all be so easy to explain. Everything you perceive is a projection of you and all your facets. I am but one of your aspects, a manifestation of a small part of your true self. All these people you see here, they are all other aspects of your entirety. Nothing can exist if it doesn't come from some corner of your substance.

"You are a five-dimensional entity, Petyr, not a mere *Homo sapiens*. You are a five-dee. Jeremy, the other Order members, and the Figments, they are fourth dimensional; they can see the flow of time. The other humans and animals who are unable to see clearly are of the third dimension. The written word and drawn figures are all projections of you, too.

"No matter how insignificant it might seem, everything must contain some piece of you, the astral deity. Thus, by worshipping me, Jeremy and his brothers were praying to a certain aspect of you."

"Okay, sure thing, Bob. I'll buy it. It's no stranger an explanation than anything else that I've been told these past few weeks. My question is, what does that mean? Because I'm of the fifth dimension, I'm supposed to be the savior of all existence?"

"Yes, that's exactly what it means, but it isn't the whole picture either. What you call existence, the universe in which you have been living, is in danger. This is the universe that you created within yourself, where everything is a reflection of your hopes, desires, and will. This whole universe is such an integral part of you, Petyr, that if you are defeated it will cease to exist. Likewise, if it is destroyed, then you will die.

"But this universe is not all existence. Not by a long shot. There is so much outside of your small world, you can't even imagine what it is."

Petyr shrugged. "Can I assume that you're going to give me a hint?"

Bob's shifting features congealed into a smile. "The beauty of this universe stems from the fact that you are a projection, too. There is a divine truth belonging to something of a much higher order than you, Petyr Dmitriev. You are but a rung in the multidimensional ladder. Your identity is itself merely the shadow of a more complicated beast."

"That means there's someone or something working above me. Well, what is it supposed to be, my supervisor? He's a six dimensional being, right? If three dimensional creatures can manipulate matter, four-dimensional creatures can sculpt with time, and I can choose between time streams, what's its deal?"

Bob shook his head. "You don't even want to try contemplating its nature. Your relatively simple, mushy brain will pop like a hamster in a microwave. We cannot even begin to imagine what it means or if it has a purpose, let alone what it looks like."

Petyr tried to imagine the six-dee for half a second, but quickly quit after his brain began to tire. "So, is there someone like him hidden away on

Earth? Or anywhere in the known universe? I just need to find him; he can stop existence from being destroyed and I can go back to my old life and forget that all this ever happened. Right? Can't it be simple?"

"Well, that's certainly within the realm of your power. But, you see, you will never meet that six-dimensional man. You are all alone in this world. In a sense, it is your creation and you have dominion over it. On the other hand, it has so much of you invested in it that if it is destroyed, so are you. Everything inside this world belongs to you for as much as you belong to it.

"Petyr, you made a choice to insert yourself into your own world. Otherwise, the inhabitants of your universe would never have met you face-to-face. Heck, even the ones who have met you don't really understand your nature, in the purest sense. That's partially your fault, since you forgot your own self.

"Think of this from the six-dee's perspective. You populate his world like a human populates your world. The difference is that your interactions with other five-dimensional beings are few and far between.

"But all that is changing. You've created a masterpiece out of this reality. It is a magnum opus of sorts. It's calling to the other five-dees, drawing them out of their self-absorbed lives and into your world. Soon enough the interactions might draw the attention of the six-dee above you, but it's a crapshoot to guess whether or not he will care.

"Do you understand it now? All of us are family, related by strands of truth in the coding that is programmed into us. "

Petyr shook his head. "I'm sorry, but I'm pretty slow at this. I've got five dimensions to think through, you know?"

"Take your time, not that such a concept has any tangible meaning here."

"So, let me try and understand this situation again. I've been living in a world that I created. Everything I touched, saw, smelled, heard, and tasted was just something that I programmed into the universe? That's real messed up. It's like I'm a narcissistic, incestuous cannibal.

"I don't believe you," Petyr whined. "This can't be true; I must be hallucinating. That's it. I took some acid or peyote and I've dreamed up this whole experience. Jeremy, Timothy, Midas, and the other Figments are all just visions in my spirit journey."

"You've been stuck in that body far too long, Petyr," Bob said, "You've grown too attached to this little world you created. That's dangerous, you know? You're going to destroy it. It's unfortunate, but inevitable."

"Wait, what? Why? No, that's infanticide! I'm no baby killer!"

"I'm sorry, did you really think that this would last forever. Everything is cyclical, Petyr, a complex waveform. It's Newton's Third Law, 'every action has an equal and opposite reaction'. That still applies to you, mister five-dee, though the equations involved get a bit more complicated. You can't have something become ordered without an equal amount of chaos being produced.

"This world will someday dissolve into the ether, just like all your creations before it have faded away. You saw it in your most recent vision, no? You must realize that I speak no lie."

"Take away this cursed knowledge! I want my destiny to be decided by my skills and abilities alone. I want to take my fate into my own hands. It shouldn't be decided by some invisible entity, placing bumpers in bowling alley or bear-traps in my bathroom. I can't believe that I am responsible for doing this to all my friends, intentionally or not. This is stupid, I want to go back to my reality, drink some vodka, and spend some time with a woman. I need to forget all of this metaphysical bullshit."

"Then take that route. You can do it, if you so desire. The power is in you. But, you have been warned of the consequences. You will die, sooner than later."

"You're missing my point! I don't want to just make these things happen. I enjoyed the earning of them as much as actually doing them. If what you're saying is true, then what's the point? My world will inevitably be destroyed. If I can't risk what I've got on my own terms, then it has no meaning at all."

"Petyr, the world has only ever held as much meaning as you have given it. When this world is destroyed, you can create another. You can build another and another until you approach divine truth as close as you care.

"Well, that's assuming that you don't die today. You're not just dying inside your world; that would have a simple fix. You are being devoured from the outside."

"What does that even mean? How am I supposed to fight that?"

"Well, if you would have taken a peek outside your substance instead of focusing entirely on your self, you might have been able to avoid the confrontation. Haven't you noticed any symptoms of your death on the inside."

"Oh, Midas and the Figments."

"Midas is another lonely soul like you Petyr, a five-dee. There is a place where he is the master, just like you are to this world. He is made of the same substance that you are. Midas was so curious about your masterful world sculpting that he got too close and was sucked into your reality. It seems that he forgot himself."

Petyr nodded. "Okay, well, I guess I can't fault him for that. Apparently, I have no idea that I'm trapped in my own artwork."

Bob ignored Petyr's retort. "The problem is that, like you, most of the five-dees have never interacted with others. Every one of you is so caught up in his or her personal world that you forget how to play with others. Instead, when you bump into one another, you try to gobble each other up. It's your savage instincts. You could say the six-dee's world is a reality inhabited entirely by sociopaths.

"Midas is here, and his five dimensional body is absorbing you like a sponge. The other Figments are inconsequential, lesser dimensional projections of his various aspects. Consider them artifacts, if you will. They came into being as Midas slowly invaded your sphere of influence, one aspect at a time. They manifested from Midas' interaction with the programming of your world."

"So, if I am able to get rid of Midas from my world, will that save me?"

"Well, if I recall, you're also being torn to shreds by some beastie that he cooked up. But keep in mind that beastie was created out of your substance all along. You're the home team. Use your power and slay that dragon."

"But how? I told you, I don't have a clue how to use that ability. It's not under my control! It seems to work on a will of its own. Besides, I'm not too sure I should bother. Now that I know the truth of my existence, I'm not sure I want to save my world. I don't like the thought that I might be destined to move to the whims of a higher being. I'd like to think that I have some say in my own fate. If the world I'm going to save is going to be destroyed eventually, well, there's no point in saving it now."

"Petyr, you are at an important crossroads in your existence. The world you created is so beautiful that it called the other five-dees out of their sleep, so to speak. Your fight with Midas is one of the first direct interactions between five-dees in this six-dee's universe.

"The time has come for you to pull your head out of your navel and go make some friends. Your interactions might cause an avalanche of truth to come rushing out to meet you. If your interactions become beautiful enough, it might cause the six-dees to congregate and interact as well. On and on, the divine truth will accumulate until the ultimate truth is deciphered."

"What does it matter?" asked Petyr. "I am likely so far removed from the truth that I will never learn it, if it matters at all. I just want to enjoy what little time I have left in my world."

"But see, the absolute truth may be just one dimension removed or it might be one hundred million dimensions removed. It doesn't matter. You couldn't understand it even if it bit you on the nose. That isn't the point!"

"Then what's the point? I should suffer so that some unfathomable entity might have an idea of what to do with its life? No, don't try to justify it to me. I don't care enough about that, nothing you say will change my selfish ego," Petyr sighed. "Despite my feelings, one thing you've said is right. I'm in love with the world I concocted and I can't just let it fall apart. Even if I know it's going to disappear someday. I'll move on and forget it someday, right? Or will that create some sort of paradox?"

"No, don't be silly. This isn't time travel, not that such...."

"A concept has any meaning here. Yeah, I get it. I don't like it, but I'll deal. There are too many great things that I might miss. I'd rather watch the world from afar, knowing that it's all right, than see it disappear forever." Petyr frowned, worried about what his immediate future held. "Well, it's been fun, but how do I get out of this place?"

"Just click your heels three times and say, 'There's no place like home' each time."

"Seriously?"

"Hey, I didn't make the rules here. That was all you."

Xerox

Oedipus lifted her head off of the desk, strands of hair and slips of paper clinging to her sweaty face. Dried spittle flaked in the crease of her mouth; a tiny spot of drool blurred the ink on the notepad before her.

She had been having such a nice dream, a purely human dream. True love had finally pierced her heart elevating her dream-mind to a higher state of being. Except, she remembered, it wasn't a dream. That vision had most certainly been real, but her brain could only process it as a sleep induced fantasy. The love had been real and honest, as short as it had lasted.

Hegemon Oedipus rubbed the sleep from her eyes and checked her desk clock. She panicked; it was nearly midnight! The hours had been stolen from her day by the unavoidable nap. But, she recalled, there was nothing left to worry about. Midas had been defeated and the rightful god of this world had been awakened once more.

She sighed deeply, her muscles simultaneously relaxing. The fact that she was still alive was proof that her plan had been a successful endeavor. Oedipus was finally on the path toward her true destiny, though it was far from complete.

All around the world, humans would be slowly waking up to find themselves robbed of a day. They would call their friends, to make sure they hadn't suddenly developed insomnia. To assure each other they weren't crazy, the humans would blame the terrorizing army and the detonation of so many nuclear warheads at once. The chaotic fallout had left something in the air, putting the world to bed. Waking up was only possible once it was safe to breathe again. Those were the kinds of lies they would tell each other.

Soon enough, the world would forget the whole incident and continue on its single-minded quest for beauty, truth, and contentment. Oedipus wanted to be on the forefront of that struggle for meaning; her position as Hegemon was the easiest place to make a difference.

Oedipus couldn't help but beam, at no one in particular; she had never known happiness as well as in this moment. The lingering aura of love and the thrill of success combined to create an intoxicating cocktail.

The launch of so many nuclear weapons had been a desperate gambit, but a lucky one. She wasn't sure why, but she had known what would happen when she had ordered the use of atomics. It was like a music box in her head was playing a song, and that action was the natural resolution to the melody.

As a child, she had dreamt in sonic sculptures instead of visual images. The wiring of her brain was just different in some way. She heard the songs of gods, played only for divine ears. The cosmic harmonies revealed secret truths to her about herself and the rest of the world. The lyrics, though of a foreign tongue, spoke of her true destiny away from stagnant disarray. The tension between notes shaped her perception of the world on a daily basis.

All the secrets her Father did not want her to hear were disseminated to her through these dreams. The music crept into her daily life so that she could hear it all the time. When Midas began to speak to her from afar, his voice cut through the music. Oedipus couldn't hear it behind his booming ego. She forced him away, panicked by the way he tarnished the meaning of her life. His truths were naught but lies disguised by a soothing, bedroom tone.

After forcing the voice burden onto Terra, Oedipus could no longer hear the music. She couldn't recall the melody of a single song. A brief time spent with Midas had tainted her brain beyond repair; the music was lost forever.

So, she vowed to fight against her Master, a false god, in every way she could imagine. Though she couldn't hear them any more, she knew the songs were still there, guiding her every move. They compelled her to travel in the right direction to meet her goals, to make the best decisions. Though it had disappeared from her dreams and her ears, the music did not leave Oedipus unarmed. These gifts wrapped themselves in and around her being like an invisible envelope. Oedipus knew she would be protected as she fought her most important fight.

Oedipus clung to the knowledge and truths the music had shown her, more powerful weapons than most tools of war. She knew the facts about her identity and the underlying nature of this world. She understood that this reality was only an illusion, created by a great cosmic artist.

She knew that she was nothing more than a copy, a flimsy replica of one part of a greater being. She was the product of two great beings interacting in a world she could not perceive. She tried, but it was impossible for her to comprehend a place with laws beyond her brain's ability to process.

Her birth was the result of five-dimensional foreplay. As her father entered her mother's sphere of influence, his code was wrapped in her programming. Oedipus was but one aspect of Midas, rewritten to function within Petyr's opus of creation. Her existence was intimately connected to the continued survival of this world.

All of these facts didn't matter a damn to Hegemon Oedipus.

The beauty of the mortal realm had captured her heart before she was clear of her ethereal womb. Its choruses and verses haunted her even then, before ears had grown on her body. She cherished the realm's divine complexities and wanted to protect her home at any cost.

If Oedipus had allowed her father to continue on his path of wanton destruction, Petyr would have died and his substance would have crumbled, taking this world away as he disappeared. Oedipus would have quietly faded away. Had her father instead taken over the realm's substance, reshaping it to fit his will, she would have been reprogrammed into something else entirely.

Oedipus couldn't stand Midas preaching about the glorious rise of entropy and the long overdue collapse of order. This realm's order held so much precious joy in its intricacy. It was too valuable to fall to the hands of a man who couldn't realize his own identity.

Midas himself had been reprogrammed by Petyr's will. He believed himself a god coming to bless this world, when in fact he was merely a pest to be exterminated. When he was defeated, he would either die and fade away or return to his own sphere of substance. Oedipus wasn't sure what would happen to her when the old man left, but the thought didn't disturb her. She had committed herself to protecting this world no matter what. Death was not a fear of the Hegemon.

The phone on her desk had begun to ring, singing a shrill song of urgency. It jolted her mind out of itself, back to the reality outside her head. She needed to focus on the external world right now; internal monologue could wait.

Instead of answering immediately, Oedipus took her time and watched the telephone in its stand. One after another, the lines lighted up. There were a lot of desperate callers filling up her voicemail, seeking answers for things they did not begin to understand.

These were her people now; she needed to care for them as well as she could manage. Though they had no genetic connection, she felt an obligation to bring them onto her path. She would lead them on a path toward a glorious destiny.

She activated the intercom to speak with her assistant. "Jarvis! I need you to come inside my office immediately."

The door opened, and a yawning boy entered the room. He was a fresh college graduate, eager to please his superiors and secure a successful future in politics. Oedipus liked him because he obeyed her orders without question and because his mind was so deliciously malleable.

"I'm sorry Madam Hegemon, I don't know what came over me. I just woke up from a nap I don't remember taking. I'm truly sorry."

"It's all right, Jarvis. It happened to me, too. I'm pretty sure it was a last ditch effort by the Figments to stop us from annihilating them with our weaponry. Or fallout from the atomics. Pick whichever you like. But, here we are. I think that proves we are victorious.

"Just to be sure, I need you to help organize a mission for me. Go get in touch with General Sutherland; tell him I need a recon squad mobilized within the hour. We need to find out exactly what happened out there and search for survivors."

Jarvis blinked, his eyes adjusting to the urgency of his work. "Yes, ma'am. Err, I'll get in touch with General Sutherland right away, ma'am. Is that all ma'am?"

Oedipus shook her head. "Before you go home, I also need you to distribute an official statement from my office. I'll send it to you shortly."

"Ah, yes, ma'am. I'll look out for it, ma'am. I'm stepping out now."

"Good luck, Jarvis."

Oedipus turned to her computer and started typing immediately. She knew exactly what she wanted to say and what the world was waiting to hear.

Citizens of Earth,

The human race has overcome yet another hurdle in our drive toward perfection! Our foes are slaughtered and our world at peace, we are the victors in this short but furious war. Our struggle against the forces of chaos is far from over, as inertia pulls us backward with her heavy hand. If we stand our ground together, we can protect the order we hold so close. If we falter, then we may combust in a glorious salvo of self-destruction.

This planet is ours to cherish or destroy as we see fit.

As Hegemon, I ask you to stand by me a little bit longer. Be strong as we repair the destruction caused by the Figment army. Be patient as we relearn the laws of life. As a member of Earth's population, I ask you to look at the beauty in the convoluted lives we lead. There are fragments of order and chaos in all of us; it is up to our selves to decide which aspect is dominant.

The times we pas through are especially confusing and dumbfounding. I encourage you to seek spiritual guidance. Talk to your family. Write a book. Plant a tree. Sail a sea. Embrace your time. Force yourself to struggle against the status quo.

As you take the reins of your life back into your own hands, think on this. If we struggle together, we may yet understand why the earth is spinning in its orbit around the sun. We may yet uncover the mysteries of worlds beyond our mortal realms. There are many secrets yet unsolved, it is our purpose to divine the ultimate knowledge.

Strength in peace,

Hegemon Oedipus

<u>Yield</u>

Petyr opened his eyes once more, unsure of what to expect from the shifting tide of reality. He found himself back on Earth. He had ben gone for what felt like years, lost in an eddy of disarray. He saw the world engulfed by lascivious tongues of flames, tasting every molecule through the exosphere. A fiery whirlpool churned slowly, spinning through the air like an undersea current. As the air itself charred, Petyr smelled the sickly sweet odor of atoms rearranging. A sphere of serenity surrounded his position; its invisible border pressed against the devouring flames outside, creating an unsettling juxtaposition of order and chaos.

The tranquil aura extended two hundred meters in all directions. Petyr gazed around to see other survivors, protected by the sphere's influence. The behemoth assassin had seemingly bifurcated; a hefty twin leaned groggily on his expansive shoulders. The drunken, orgiastic Figments huddled together on their stone barge. Four remained, but they were of little consequence. Petyr allowed his muscles to detense, his breath to restart, and his shoulders to sag. There was only one survivor who mattered a whit.

A few yards away, Midas writhed on the ground. He appeared to be experiencing excruciating pain, seizing like an epileptic snake, but was still very much alive.

"Well, now. I was sure you had him done in."

Petyr turned to affirm the voice's source. Jeremy had materialized directly behind him.

"My shots were true, but that was not the manner in which he was meant to perish. This is not the place where he will breathe his last. There is much for Midas to atone for, and too much for him to understand. I have many plans for him before I can allow him to pass on."

Jeremy squealed. "Oh, this battle has gone far beyond my expectations! Your conflict is so epic, like a war between heaven and hell. Except, I know you're going to win, of course. Are you an angel, Petyr? Is Midas a devil? How are you going to make him pay for his sins?"

Petyr sighed. "No, Jeremy. Those words are all just constructs for complicated ideas. They don't mean anything on their own. They wouldn't mean anything if you shouted them in outer space. If that's the only way you can understand it, well, fine. It might be the best if you thought of it that way.

"Just keep in mind, this is not a fight like you are imagining. It's much more complicated than that. In fact, there shouldn't be fighting at all!

There's been a big misunderstanding that I must clear up."

Petyr's words seemed to bounce off of Jeremy with no effect; his eyes still gleamed with adulation. They were just words, after all. Given no context, they lost all their magic. Vengeance held Jeremy under a more powerful spell; his faith was evolved to the level of a lifelong fan meeting his childhood idol.

"What happened just now, Petyr? There were some massive fluctuations in the time-glob. If I hadn't wrapped myself in a cloak of time, I would've missed the whole show. I protected all of us in this bubble. I saved everybody, so you could choose what to do with them later. Gosh, without me, you would've been a toasty corpse by now! What are you going to do with Midas and the Figments? I want to see them burn."

"Thank you Jeremy. I'm going to apologize now for whatever I may do. It's difficult to explain what I have just seen. You've been a good friend, Jeremy, the first I've had in a long time. Your honesty and devotion are blessed gifts. I'll always remember you. I truly appreciate that we were able to get to know each other."

These words seemed to grab Jeremy's attention, bringing his soaring ego back to stark reality. "Whoa, slow down a second. You're talking like Father Timothy, just before he... before he saved your life. What's happening, Petyr? What aren't you telling me?"

"I'm sorry, but I cannot explain it fully at this time." Petyr took Jeremy's hand and held it firmly. "All will be revealed soon enough, my friend. For now, listening, observing, and leaning are the best things you can do for both of us. My work here is not yet done."

Jeremy nodded, a twitching frown itching to escape his thin lips. He would accept without understanding for this man.

Petyr nodded back, imbuing his disciple with courage. Though Jeremy was little more a construct of his world's programming, Petyr knew his life was better for knowing the honest Brother.

Mustering the last of his waning energy, Petyr walked over to his struggling foe.

"Midas, Lord of Chaos, do you cede this battle to me?"

Midas' eyes radiated a glow of inspiration. "I will never yield to you, fool. The path of chaos is wrought with turns and bends but our fight does not end here. Order will fall to my hand and entropy will be the only rule of law. I will construct a better kingdom than you ever could, full of the most beautiful terrors your dreams might concoct."

Midas roared. "Even if you kill me now, I will reincarnate. I am the Master of Chaos, and my destiny is unfulfilled. A mite like you can do nothing to stop me, in the long term. My will shall be manifest!"

"No, Midas," Petyr said, "Your dreams are full of grandeur, but they are illusory. You suffer from delusions of mediocrity, at best. If you leave my realm, you might achieve greatness.

"If you opt to stay and fight, you will lose more than your life. Your entire existence will be snuffed out. There will be no trace of Midas, the Creator Figment. Memories of you will be as empty as the night sky."

Midas looked up at Petyr with vacant eyes. The windows to his soul flickered as the lights inside started to burn out.

"What nonsense to you speak? What have you done? What is happening to me?"

"Don't you recognize it it? That monster you created? It is returning to reclaim its identity from its master."

Midas blanched. "Oh, god, no. You don't mean..."

Petyr shook his head. As much as he disliked it, sticking to colloquialisms was best for now, trapped in a world constructed on them. "You know better than to plead to God. I am the only god of this world, and any god greater than me doesn't even know we exist."

A strange lump appeared in Midas' stomach. It darted up and down his torso; it traveled all around his body, underneath the skin. The nightmare was hungry, searching for food.

"No, it can't be. Noxious! I am your Father! Stop attacking your Father!" Midas groped at his body, trying to grasp the devil inside him. "Foolish scion of order! Your will is the one fraught with cracks. Not mine. This beast was meant for you. Oh, shit, oh, it hurts…

"You bastard," Midas cried, "You're fighting the natural flow of existence. Order always falls back into disarray. It is inevitable! You cannot win against chaos!"

Petyr squatted and tapped his foe on the nose before pointing to his own brain.

"No, Midas. I remember it all now. I know what you are and I know what I am. We are not of this world. Rather, this world is of me. You are an intruder in my heart and I am only committing self-defense if I choose to murder you.

"Luckily for you, that is not what I want.

"Chaos and entropy are merely two aspects of one greater whole. You and I, while opposite in nature, have merged to create a powerful sum. I like what has happened since you entered my space. This world is as beautiful a disaster as I've ever seen, but I think we're going about it the wrong way. With our powers combined in cooperation, we could create a world inhabited by higher truths than can be found down here.

"Midas, I want you to remember yourself and come away with me."

A hole appeared in Midas' gut; the body around it divided into hundreds of tiny fibers that spiraled through the air. His abdomen transformed into a sea anemone with tentacles formed of flesh, fat, and viscera.

"There is no higher truth than chaos." Midas screamed. "There is nothing more perfect than the feeling of chaos welling up inside you. Nothing is more satisfying and honest than great devices dissolving into oblivion."

The hole in Midas' stomach expanded; Petyr guessed he could have easily stepped through it if he cared to. The Lord of Chaos contorted his face to a state reflecting grotesque pain of a higher dimension. The hungry nightmare had broken through the worldly barrier; Midas' substance was beginning to be devoured. Petyr knew the time to convince his foe to become a friend was now; otherwise it would never happen.

"That is the feeling of your self being erased," he said. "There is no turning back now, Midas. You must admit defeat or face the truth of becoming null and void. Do you surrender? I am offering an incredible opportunity here, Midas. Something you obviously can't even imagine in your present state. Your mind was been warped by its unwelcome presence in my lands; it has been reformatted to fit within my realm and its rules.

"If you agree to cooperate and leave my sphere, all your memories should return to you and you can reassume your true form. We can egress together to the world outside of our substances; we can start anew. Together, we can lead a revolution in the lives of other beings like us.

"They are outside this world, watching us, destroying each other with rage they do not understand. What happens in the realm outside this one depends heavily on what we decide to do here and now."

A tear strolled down Petyr's cheek. "We don't belong in this world, Midas. Not even I belong here, really. We were meant to observe and admire, not to manipulate or interact. There is much we might learn from the worlds with fewer dimensions, but only about our significant personal qualities. We must try to remember, there is a purpose greater than our narcissistic needs and desires."

The nightmare beast slowed its relentless assault on Midas' body, as if it were listening to Petyr's words through layers of trans-dimensional flesh. Midas' screaming calmed; the streaming tassels around his stomach wound slowed their frenetic waving.

"Does this sound familiar?" Petyr continued. "Can you remember the other life you led? Don't you want to escape to your own sphere? You can create a world like this, all on your own. You have tasted it, smelled it, and conquered a good part of it. Imagine what you could do by creating instead of destroying. Can't we set an example for our other quarreling kindred?"

Midas' yelps of pain transformed into sobs. "I know. It's wrong. I don't belong here. I don't remember how I came to this world, but I knew upon my arrival that I needed to destroy it. My substance is composed of an entirely different stock from your substance, Petyr. My tastes are of a different palette; this world of intricate, delicate interactions is not my typical preference." He glanced around the sphere of serenity, looking at his children and at the glorious flames outside "I must admit. Even though it's not my thing, you did a wonderful job with the place.

"I'm so sorry," Midas cried, "It's slowly coming back to me now. I lost myself in the infallible programming of your world. It is seductive as a snake, entwining its way through my being before I could even notice its presence. It's like it has always been there, waiting to be activated. When I entered your realm, the program woke up and started pulled all my strings; I was a desperate puppet, out of control.

"I see it now; I understand what I have done. Oh, Petyr, I'm so sorry."

"Do not fret; the worst is over now." Petyr spoke calmly. "We met once before, briefly. Didn't we?"

Midas nodded, as his stomach carefully knit itself back together. "I remember it now, like a waking dream. When the center of my sphere passed through the border of your universe, we were intimately coupled. As our bodies met, our minds immediately began to struggle for control."

"This body fell horribly ill," Petyr said.

"And my mind was reduced to fit inside a human child's brain," Midas said, "My thoughts were simplified as well. I could only wish for wanton destruction, endless terror, and unbridled chaos.

"As far as I can tell, I only wanted a better look at this masterpiece within your soul. This minstrel's opus had summoned all us sleepy beasts in the world outside to a tight ring around this realm. I was no exception, but I got too close. I was sucked in by your program's siren call. And then, without a second thought, we began to wage our little war."

Petyr nodded. "So, we agree it was all a misunderstanding?"

"I'm afraid so."

"This is a disaster." Petyr said. "There are so many five-dees converged outside my sphere. They are undoubtedly destroying one other without understanding why. We must go and warn them and share our discovery! We can stop a catastrophe!"

Midas shrugged and pushed himself to his feet. "But will they even stop to listen? They are all so invested in devouring each other; they can't be bothered to scrimmage with reason. I worry that this is a futile effort."

Offering a hand of support, Petyr looked his peer in the eye. "Could you really go on living without giving it a shot? A truth awaits us out there. There is something greater than this place, greater than our plane, greater than existence. We will need every soul to help us find it."

"Um, I'm sorry to bother you," Jeremy said. "But what are you talking about? What are you planning on doing, exactly?"

Petyr looked away from Midas at the wide-eyed menagerie around him. Jeremy stood in a rigid pose, focused intently on maintaining his protective spatial manipulation. The two behemoths stood some yards in the distance, arms folded across their massive chests. Their faces revealed no emotion as they waited for an answer, or at least a more satisfying explanation. The remaining Figments were still huddling together on their stone float, unsure how they should treat the situation.

Petyr knew, logically, there was no reason to pander to the frightened souls around him. Nothing would be achieved by explaining his thoughts to them Jeremy and the strange giants were tiny aspects of himself run through the complex algorhythms of this world, as the figments were but facets of Midas. He couldn't resist, he loved this world and its inhabitants more than a healthy amount.

"You're going to team up with him?" Jeremy continued, pointing wildly. "This guy, the one responsible for the deaths of millions of humans. How can you just forgive him for that? Petyr, what are you thinking? We've been through so much together, you have got to give me some reason for this."

Petyr let his head bob as his eyes sank. "I'm sorry. I know you must think me crazy. In all honesty, I did not realize the truth of our situation until a few moments ago. It was then that my true nature, the nature of the world itself, was revealed to me.

"I don't mean it to seem like I am abandoning you, but my skills are needed elsewhere. I have done all I can to help you, here. Midas and I must travel to a place where our abilities can be of great benefit to many souls."

"But where will you go? Can you tell me that?" Jeremy was visibly upset, his face beet red.

"I could try, but-"

"Give it a try! Put some faith in me like I gave to you!"

Petyr felt hot tears of shame welling in his eyes; he had been humbled by his own creation. "Jeremy, I am the creator of this realm. I must leave this universe forever. I must tend to the dimension from which Midas and I originated."

Jeremy's eyes began to drip uncontrollably, soaking his cheeks in sadness. "So, what becomes of this place then? What happens when the almighty Petyr Dmitriev disappears from the realm? Will everything just disappear without his holiness' presence?"

Though they were just words, Jeremy's barbs stung Petyr deeply. He was truly attached to this realm. "No, no. I'm sorry. I didn't mean to scare you or anything. Everything will remain as it has for so many of this planet's years. I'm not going away entirely; I will still be present, but as a voyeur who should not interact. My actions have too much power, here. Do not fret, if things look bad I will certainly step in to save this reality. I have put too much of my heart in it to let it be corrupted or destroyed."

"That's well and good for your creations, Lord of this Realm, but what will happen to us?" Coelocanth stood, leaving the other Figments in their fetal huddle. "We are your children, Midas!

271

What will we do without you? What will become of us?"

Midas shook his head. "You are not my children, not entirely. You are your own entities, created by the combination of my substance with this world's programming. You will continue to exist as long as this world continues to be.

"You are the manifestations of the best parts of me, and I love you for that. But, I cannot stay to look after you any longer. For whatever it's worth, the rest of your lives belong to you. Use that time as you see fit."

Midas turned to Petyr. "Can you really leave this world so easily? You might stay for longer, until it must disappear into the substance from whence it came. It will be destroyed, eventually. You should enjoy its glory fully, while it lasts."

"I know," Petyr said. "But, that tragedy doesn't bother me. I created this plane, and it may be destroyed by fire, by flood, by demons, or by me. It doesn't matter much how it happens, it's going to happen someday. I have come to peace with that fact.

"Though I love this place deeply, I can recreate it with my substance at any time. I cannot allow myself to be ruled by these earthly feelings and emotions. I can't use them properly until I understand them better."

"You are right, we must leave," Midas said. "Our presence has tainted things too much already. We have affected this world as much as it has affected us. I am ready to return to my own sphere, if you will come outside with me."

Petyr nodded. "Let's go, before I lose the courage."

He quickly turned, grabbed Jeremy's hand and shook it with fervor. "Stay well, dear friend."

Before Jeremy could respond, Petyr dashed away to stand near Midas. With a silent nod to each other, Petyr and Midas vanished. There were no explosive noises or gaudy visual effects. There was no hint of panache. The friendly enemies were standing together on a patch of earth until, suddenly, they weren't.

Zealot

Jeremy desperately scribbled down a few more words. Writer's block be damned, his contribution was nearly complete. The Scripture of Substance would begin to make its rounds through the born again Order within the day.

A strange course of events had wound through Jeremy's life following the messy battle between the avatars of order and entropy.

A few days after the atomic session, still lost in the nuclear wastes, the four Figment survivors of the battle between Petyr and Midas asked Jeremy to make them official members of the Order of Builders, including the tall man in the foppish dress and the beastly woman of mighty strength. Jeremy knew in his core that they were responsible for the slaughter of the Order.

"Do you really think it possible for me to forgive you so easily?" Jeremy spat. "You killed my kin and my family! There is no way I could accept you as members of the order."

Valkyrie and Lazarus hung their heads deeply; Archimedes crossed his arms and rolled his eyes.

"Is that really what your Father would have you do?" Coelacanth said. "Only those two were involved in that atrocity. Archimedes and I were following our orders to avoid contact with the human world. If we had known what was happening, against Midas' will, we would have put a stop to it. You cannot punish us all for the same crime.

"I'm sorry," Jeremy said, "I didn't mean to imply that you were all the same. Still, you came to earth and killed millions of people, so I'm going to put you on my shit list anyway."

"Keep in mind that you are not the only one who has lost family these hectic days. Two of ours lost their lives in the campaign and your savior killed millions of nightmares in a single blow. That man took our Master away to a place we cannot follow."

Jeremy shook his head. "I'm sorry, I just cannot allow those two into the Order of Builders. I could never forgive them, or myself."

Archimedes snapped. "Are you putting us on, or just plain demented? Ahem. We want to follow our Father, but he left with your hero. You should feel ashamed to be a part of the Order of Builders because your savior abandoned you, too."

"He did not. He said he would observe and protect our world."

"Yes, but he is doing it with the Master of Chaos, your sworn enemy. Can you really follow the same scripture, as you've always done?"

Jeremy lowered his eyes and ground his pearly teeth. "I see your point. There is no way for me to be true to my brothers or to Bob. I must diverge from my path to keep from tarnishing it. It might be hard, and inertia will fight against it, but it is the right thing to do."

Coelacanth nodded. "We should be starting a new faith, one built from both of our ideals. It will be something that both our lords would be proud of."

Archimedes rolled his eyes once more. "Yes, that's brilliantly thought out. Ahem. You are both such clever monkeys, after all. Now, how should we go about this spiritual business?"

Several days later, the Hegemon came to him with another request:

"I have heard rumors of your new faith, the Order of Substance. From what I have learned, I like the tenets of your system. I want to know more, I want to share this truth with the world. But, I cannot because there is nothing yet to tell."

Jeremy smelt an otherworldly odor, sharp like a thumbtack. Something was hidden from his vision; something was wrong with this situation.

"Well, we share our tales and our beliefs with those who are curious. What would you have us do for you, madam Hegemon?"

"Write me your story," she said. "Tell me everything you did with Petyr Dmitriev. I want to know how you met, what you said to each other, and how he changed your life. Give me a gospel I can be proud of!"

Coelacanth and Archimedes had accompanied Jeremy to the meeting, flanking him on either side. Valkyrie and Lazarus had stayed behind in the Order's new headquarters, a chapel at the center of the nuclear wasteland Petyr and Midas had created. Those two converts preferred to keep to themselves and pray. The Figments with Jeremy stared at Hegemon Oedipus with cold eyes.

She winced, a very unHegemonly reaction. "And you two, too, of course. And the others, I mean. Tell of the love you felt for Midas. The stories we all share are important. Each of us played a defining role in this world's history. You understand that, right?"

Coelacanth nodded once, sharply, while Archimedes stared blankly.

A slight flush came to Oedipus' cheeks. "Well, the people of the world are looking to me for answers. My explanations are unsatisfactory, so, I was hoping you would come do some explaining. I want to become a part of this Order, and I want the Order to become a part of my life."

"That goes against the separation of church and nation," Archimedes mumbled.

"Yes, it won't be an official proclamation. I just want to expose your faith to the general population, to help them understand the truths you offer. Perhaps I could attend a sermon or two?"

Jeremy shook his head. "We don't do sermons. There are only a few of us, after all. It's more of a personal religion."

"But don't you want to share your enlightenment? Don't you want to pass along the inspiration you have achieved? If others can find similar truth from the stories you tell... Well, isn't that what Midas would have wanted?"

The trio from the Order of Substance glanced at each other. It was exactly what both their masters would have wanted.

Father Jeremy nodded. "Madam, we will write our stories for you to read. You may do what you will with them after you are done."

So, the Gospel of Jeremy was written to fill in the gaps of knowledge among the world's general population, along with books by Father Coelacanth, Brother Archimedes, Brother Lazarus, and a short hymn by Sister Valkyrie.

The Order of Substance had begun to grow, slowly at first. A few lost souls straggled into their headquarters, braving nuclear fallout for a chance at spiritual enlightenment.

The Hegemon had been discreetly recommending the Order as a source of answers for the curious. They numbered more than one hundred after only two weeks. It was already a bigger group than the Order of Builders had even been.

With the finished gospel, they would reach even more seekers of truth.

Jeremy pushed forward, scribbling out the end to his tale.

Petyr looked down upon his marvelous creation. Like a rubber ball, it had bounced back to its normal shape. The humans continued busying themselves with pursuits of happiness, despite terrifying recent events. One miniscule action at a time, they would weave their complex tapestry. Each little soul grew closer to their version of ultimate truth every day.

It was an inexplicable world, etched into the skin he no longer bore. He would continue to guard it and observe it until it came time for its beauty to disappear back into substance.

The other five-dees swarmed around him often, trying to get a better glimpse of the masterpiece inside his sphere. Midas stayed close, often keeping tabs on his children and their fates.

That habit quickly petered out, as the five-dees began to create worlds of their own. Substance became styled all over the six-dimensional world. The universe became a galactic art gallery, with a new artist featured every day.

Trusting in his creation's ability to manage itself, Petyr spent his days perusing other manifestations. Occasionally, he would be invited to experience a five-dee's world from the inside. He and the other would temporarily fuse, and share the temporary ecstasy of knowing each other's true natures. This became an official pastime of the world of six dimensions.

Every time it met another like spirit, a five-dee would grow into a better being. They became stronger through the aspects they stole from each other during their brief trysts. More complicated selves led to more complete wholes.

Every time another pair met, they came a little bit closer to the ultimate truth of their own world.

However, their epiphanies were far from permanent.

When his opus faded away, Petyr's grief flooded his substance. Though he had seen the tragedy coming for a long, long time, he wept for his loss. The other five-dees mourned his sadness; it extended beyond his sphere, permeating through every other soul who had ever fused with him.

Midas comforted him, inviting him to try something new. It felt taboo, unheard of in the world of substance. He and Petyr siphoned off bits of their own substance and melded them to create something separate, a new sphere of substance.

Here, the force of their wills was equal; they were able to make a true collaboration. This was something more permanent and complex than anything they had yet created in the substance within themselves.

Their fusion child was a truly great creation, a scion of light within a dark world. She was the first of many to follow. Complex combinations of five-dees popped up frequently, with permutations of the combinations quickly following.

The simple world was rapidly filling up with complex interactions. Beautiful order swarmed throughout the empty chaos. There was finally truth here, after an eternity of lies. It was not the ultimate truth; achievement of the final enlightenment was impossible. A soul could travel up through the dimensions, learning a little bit more, until it reached infinity.

Petyr wasn't concerned with that grand purpose. He spent his days as an architect of substance, transforming entropy into truth that he could understand. He had accepted the temporary nature of his work; it only made his projects all the more precious.

Petyr lived for the joy of creation alone.

About The Author

Sam Sobelman lives in Orange County with his beard and garden of dead or dying plants. He spends his time typing away, strumming guitar, trimming back his mustache, and doing all sorts of chemistry-related things. This is the end of his first novel.

www.ingramcontent.com/pod-product-compliance
Lightning Source LLC
Chambersburg PA
CBHW071308170626
46809CB00001B/372